INTO THE DANGEROUS WORLD

Books by Julie Chibbaro

Redemption

Deadly

Into the Dangerous World

INTO THE DANGEROUS WORLD

julie chibbaro
art by JM SUPERVILLE SOVAK

VIKING

VIKING
An Imprint of Penguin Random House LLC
375 Hudson Street
New York, New York 10014

First published in the United States of America by Viking,
an imprint of Penguin Random House LLC, 2015

LIBRARY OF CONGRESS CATALOGING-IN-PUBLICATION DATA IS AVAILABLE
ISBN: 978-0-803-73910-9

Printed in the USA

10   9   8   7   6   5   4   3   2   1

Design by Jim Hoover

This story happens in a fictional New York City, some of which existed,
some of which never did.

The art was done in India ink, graphite, watercolor, spray paint, Sharpie, Design Markers,
and collage on Strathmore paper. The display type is Vinyl OT, the text was set in Manti-
core, and some portions are hand-lettered.

For Samsa

"I too am not a bit tamed."

—WALT WHITMAN

"Graffiti is an art, and if art is a crime,
please God, forgive me."

—LEE QUIÑONES, ARTIST

"If this is art, then to hell with art."

—ALFRED OLIVERI, HEAD OF THE NEW YORK
CITY TRANSIT AUTHORITY'S VANDAL SQUAD

1

THE NIGHT DADO burned down our house, he came upstairs and into my room. In his arms, he cradled a thick roll of brown butcher paper that he must have bought near the chemical plant where he worked. He smelled of sulfur, like a lit match. I hunched over my sketches on the wood floor, drawing the serrated edge of a knife, sharp and ready for a heart. I always drew on the floor, my paper spread out around me. There was no other space on our whole four acres that could contain me.

When Dado came in, he set down the paper and kicked it. We didn't say anything, watching it roll out. He towered over me, and I couldn't tell which Dado he was. He wore his combat boots and seemed jittery. Across the room, the paper stopped with a bump under the window. I didn't know what he wanted me to do with it—a wrong move could set him off.

"I'm going to save you, girl," he said.

I looked up just as he turned away and walked back out.

With my charcoal, I got my hand gliding across that paper like I had centuries of time and miles of surface to cover. Lately, Dado had been spending nights downstairs alone in his armchair reading Blake's God visions and studying those wild drawings of dancing people. He kept close watch on our dome house on the edge of the Kill, on a property once filled with people who danced just like in the Blake drawings. People who left one by one until it was just me and him, Ma, and Marilyn.

I heard a shout.

No, I didn't hear anything, that's what happened. The fire blazed quietly.

Dado built that dome house with his own callused, blackened hands and with boards he hauled from the landfill. He hammered it together with nails he pulled from old planks and straightened. Together, we formed the triangle struts with two-by-fours, bolted them in rows around the perimeter until we had a second story, until the apexes made a five-pointed star. We fitted the last five triangles together as a pentagon. Over it all, we nailed the plywood and framed glass, closing it in from the rain.

I didn't hear the crackling downstairs, the fire eating the dried wooden walls, the beams, the floors we had laid. Ma and Marilyn were making too much noise arguing in the sewing room, that's what happened. Through my wall, I could hear only my big sister's angry voice: "He's crazy, you know that. We should go, Ma, like the others—let's just go." If she had shut up for one minute, I would have heard.

I didn't know how long Dado was downstairs, burning.

Then Ma and Marilyn burst into my room, choking, coughing—smoke billowing in with them. The flames behind Ma petrified me.

"Open the window, Ror, get out, *get out!*" she shouted.

I couldn't think or move. Loudest thing going through my head was *My drawings!* Years, boxes of notebooks, sketchpads, zines, album covers. Ma threw my chair and smashed the window and shoved Marilyn through the hole. Flames licked the walls of my room. I could feel them melting my wool sweater, the back of my pants, my canvas sneakers. I smelled burning hair. My hair.

"Dado! Where's Dado?" I cried.

Ma came back for me.

I felt a searing up my neck, the burning; my throat seized. Ma slapped at me and grabbed me by the arm and yanked me up until I stood. She thrust me across the room; I plowed through the broken window, the glass catching my ear as I leaped toward the oak tree and slid down. Ma burst out and fell into the snow behind me, where Marilyn lay bleeding. I shivered, the sirens sounding far away, my skin howling.

I knew he was still inside.

Flames covered the whole dome. Fire trucks came finally,

with pumped-up firemen who took one glance at us, then got straight to work. They slammed forced water from the tank into the outside walls, but it wasn't enough to stop the fire. There were no hydrants. We lived in the boonies, homesteading on discarded land. If only I could move my limbs, if only I could let go of the wails.

Ma shouted at the fire, *"Peter, Peter!"* Orange light reflecting in Marilyn's eyes gave her a wild look. I backed away from them, a snowball to my torn ear, that dark March night swallowing me. My sister clutched my mother, their teeth chattering. I felt like I had nothing to hold on to, like I couldn't reach them.

An ambulance came. Somebody in uniform threw a coat around me as the medics hurried toward me. I heard, "Back up, everybody, it's gonna go!"

Fire whooshed up as the dome collapsed in with a crash.

Dado said he was going to save me, but I didn't know what he meant. Staring at the thundering orange blaze, I thought I could have saved him somehow. Anger rushed up like the flames over the dome—I didn't care. I thought I didn't care. I thought that's how I felt. For him to destroy himself and all we had created, I didn't care.

I don't know Dado, I thought in a panic. *I don't know what his face looks like.* If I wanted to remember him, I'd have to draw fast.

2

THE COLD HALL clanged with rolling beds. A nurse took my pulse—I didn't want to be here, I'd never been to a hospital, not once, not even when I cut into my thigh with the chain saw, taking down the maple sapling. I bawled and shrieked while Dado tied the tourniquet—"Think of the guys who walk across coals, who lie on beds of nails. Beat the pain, girl, beat the pain," he'd said. Ma sewed the cut and spread on mashed garlic against infection. Blood seeped through the black stitches. I smelled like garlic for days, but it healed. I didn't need to be in this hospital.

The gauze around my tender head seemed too tight, the pain causing little blue sparks to dance in the center of my mind. My ear throbbed. Across the way, Ma sat with Marilyn, who had three fingers splinted together. Despite the fire, and jumping out the window, and a busted left hand, my sister's chestnut hair was still in a neat ponytail at the base of her neck. Ma's eyes were bleak, her black hair wild. A pig came and talked to her. "They want to release you. There ain't nothin' left down there. Chief says I can't let you go back. The whole area is condemned. You got somebody I could call?" he asked. His shoulders looked slack and dumb—Dado always said you could never trust a pig.

Ma said, "We don't want to go back. There's no going back for us."

He sighed, like he didn't know what else to do. "Yeah, so, can't you think of a name of one person I can call for youse?"

Ma glared at him—I could read her thoughts—was he grilling her for info about the commune? "No."

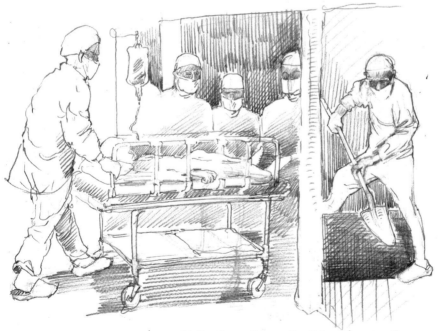

HOSPITALS ARE WHERE PEOPLE GO TO DIE.

The cop glanced over at me, shivering on my gurney. I thought of Dado's pot plants in the back field. The man's voice softened. "There's nobody we can call to help you?"

"I said, there's no one," she repeated, her voice hard.

There was no one left.

Marilyn pulled Ma over, and I heard her whisper, "What about Laura's family?" Her Norm friend from school.

Ma shook her head. She said, "No. *No one.*" Her mottled face looked like a mask, like a stranger was in the emergency room with us.

I tried to think of somebody. "Gloria?" But all those people had been gone for years.

Ma whispered furiously, "Do you *really* think I would dig *them* up for anything?" I saw the thought—*They were right about him*—before she buried it.

The cop scratched his thigh, muttering something like, "Damn loco hippies," while a young nurse came over to write out some papers.

"I gotta take off, kid," he told me. "I'm gonna need the coat back."

I looked down, and with a hit of nausea, I saw the blue, the silver shield. Without meeting his eyes, I unwrapped myself and handed it over.

"Take care of yourself," he said.

I didn't answer. We sat with our papers until a woman in tight polyester came over, talking like she didn't even see us. "My name is Tammy, and I'll be your social worker. I can arrange a night in a shelter until you can get yourselves straightened out. We can place you in a mission—"

"No," Ma interrupted. "No church. We're not going anywhere near any churches."

Tammy regarded us warily, her middle-aged face set in stone. "There's no room in the Staten Island shelter. Budget cuts." When Ma folded her bone-thin arms against herself, Tammy backed down. "Okay, no church. Maybe we can find something in Brooklyn."

We followed her into an office, where she made phone calls.

They sent us to a family shelter—a converted community center with linoleum floors and flickering fluorescents. A guy brought us to the rows of cots set up on a basketball court, a hive of families rustling and snoring under sick blue lights. Felt like the tent in the early days, all of us crammed together. I slipped beneath the itchy wool blanket, but I couldn't fall asleep, listening to the ragged breathers, the baby criers, the snorers, my entire self a purple bruise of fury, my head stinging.

I couldn't forgive Dado.

Why'd you do it?

3

THE PLACE STANK of anonymous farts, pit funk, dollar perfume. I watched messed-up girls cut their forearms and shins in the bathroom with light bulb shards. Behind Dumpsters, hopeless boys got stoned on glue. Short-tempered parents reined their kids in like dogs. Marilyn took off during the day to go to school somewhere, and I kept to myself. I stole the sign-in book to draw on, the newspaper from the guard's desk to read.

If Dado saw us now—living on the man's dime, patched up and homeless—he would've cited the Manifesto, Number 3: *We vow not to depend on anyone to hand us anything.* It would have killed him, Ma asking for handouts like she was.

But it was his fault we were here.

She got herself into the office with the stiffo social worker lady, making demands. "We can't stay. We need help. We lost our house to a fire, and we need a place to live. We need money. I'll fill out whatever forms you want . . ."

I could hear her from the hall where I watched Tom chase Jerry on TV.

Television was Number 6 of the Manifesto: *We will not succumb to addictions, weakness, or self-pity—that's what the man wants. We will not let him control us through TV, heroin, alcohol, or cigarettes.*

They had a room with donated clothes. I dug out a pair of Gloria Vanderbilt jeans, death-black Doc Martens, a tight-waisted Columbia coat. A black watch cap to cover my wrecked head. It was my turn with the social worker: a sand-colored woman with pebbly skin, greasy curls, and huge plastic glasses who sat behind a desk piled with papers. She had the perfect name: Miss Gray. She gave me a form to fill out and wrote as she spoke, not looking at me. "Your mother told me what happened."

"Yeah? What happened?" I said.

She looked at her file, checking. "Your house burned down. Your father died."

What did she want me to say? I took a pen off her desk and flipped the form over and started to draw— the King Kennedys, four acres of utopian paradise Dado founded when I was two. The pond, the dome, where the chickens used to live, and the goats, before we ate them all.

"And the fire started—how?" she asked.

"How the fuck should I know?"

Her chair creaked. She slipped a handful of paper under my pen. "Show me," she said. I kept drawing—Hawk and Waterfall. Gloria. The pot field. My tools. Pressing against my thigh was the knife I'd snuck past the guard, the one treasure I'd saved from the fire. I could stab it through the paper and hold it up to her, *show* her.

She said, "You're angry, Aurora."

No shit.

"You're only hurting yourself, being so angry at him." So she knew. She knew he burned the dome down.

His last words, *"I'm going to save you, girl."* I felt her eyes leave me. I couldn't forgive, I didn't care how much I hurt myself. A heart can't forgive so easily. Think about it, lady. Draw *your* father in an armchair decorated with matches and soaked with gasoline, and animate it.

Watch him light the fire and burn down your house and everything that's important to you, everything you ever cared about in your entire life, and let me know if you forgive him, even if you love him more than anything in the whole fucking world.

Miss Gray said, "Time's up, Aurora. More tomorrow."

I stuck the paper under my coat. When she turned away, I shoved the pen in my boot and left.

4

MA AND DADO on those acres of land—that's where all this started. A couple of years after I was born. Four acres is big; you can get lost on four acres.

We came from the city. Dado brought us in the orange VW van, me and Halo and Ma, after he got beat up at an antiwar rally on Wall Street. We came with Jan and Dick, Gloria's parents. Jan was a teacher who had dropped out; Dick changed his name and faith after Watergate. Now he was Ramakrishna, named after the Hindu saint; we called him Krishna for short. Carol showed up in her green station wagon—an herbalist, a childless, patchouli-scented soul mother—with her partner Randy, a damp man who could never meet your eyes. Randy taught us how to hot-wire electricity from the pole.

All the years we were there, felt like we were always waiting

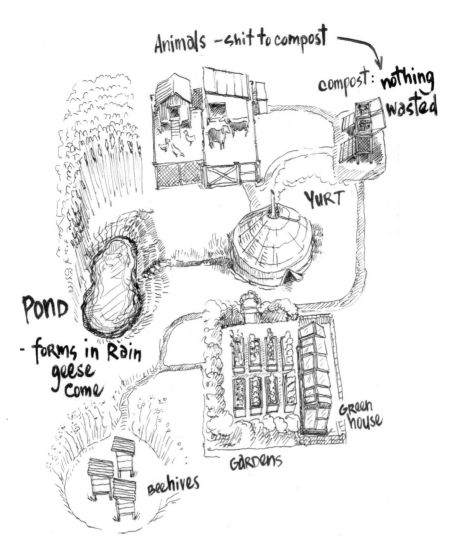

Animals —shit to compost
compost: nothing wasted
YURT
POND
- forms in Rain
geese come
Green house
Gardens
Beehives

for someone to kick us off, but nobody ever did. *Homesteading,* Dado called it. *Squatters,* what the Norms called us. I hated that word—like squirt, squeamish, like "You ain't squat."

Ray and Linda, both Black Panthers, brought their twin boys Djefa and Kean, who were Halo's age. I was the only one who knew the hidden difference between the twins—the teardrop birthmark under Djefa's right arm, the mole behind Kean's left ear. After them came Waterfall, a strawberry-blonde girl whose skin turned pink in the sun. And, finally, Hawk, who would never be seen without his fringe jacket, even during a heat wave.

Dado was in charge. He called us "the King Kennedys," after the deaths of Martin Luther Junior and John and Robert—deaths he took harder than his own parents', Ma said. Ray wrangled the animals. Hawk designed the round yurt tent. Carol took her wagon on dump runs. Krishna dug clay and threw pots. Randy managed the bees. The chickens were our job, all the kids. The fifteen of us lived in the yurt, heating it by burning scavenged wood.

Dado was big, smart, and muscular as hell. He'd studied political science. He could carry two cinder blocks on one arm. He read us Whitman, Stokely Carmichael, Tolstoy. He started writing the King Kennedys manifesto during the Nixon trials and finished it by the end of the Vietnam War, right when Ford became president. For a long time, it was just his scrawl on a piece of paper.

Then I designed the lettering. I worked for weeks, and he hung it over the hearth. It was there until we tore down the yurt.

We went in the van to No Nukes protests and concerts in Central Park. Nights around the fire, we danced to Hawk's guitar, Dado's congas, Waterfall's tambourine. Barefoot in the warmed dirt, I lost myself in the music. Dado sang in his burr-edged voice songs of peace. When everyone sold off their stuff for cash, he refused to give up his records and phonograph machine.

Communitarian Manifesto
of the King Kennedys

Live by this and make no substitute.

1. We will not let ambition cloud our love.
   Love is our connection to earth, the reason we're here.

2. We shall not be phonies. We will show our real faces.

3. We must fight for what we want and win. We vow not
   to depend on anyone to hand us anything.

4. We will build it ourselves. Each step must have a purpose.

5. We won't trust anyone. We won't need anyone.

6. We will not succumb to addictions, weakness, or self-pity
   — that's what the man wants. We will not let him control
   us through TV, heroin, alcohol, or cigarettes.

7. No sugar, No meat. They just ain't good for you.

8. No Band-aids, No Tampax. No Levi's jeans. No CocaCola.

9. Nothing is free, including love.

Ma sewed us drawstring pants and peasant shirts; she crocheted beads into necklaces and tied them on us for good luck. I played with the beads till the yarn tattered in my fingers. At the farmer's market, she sold her colorful afghans, her mojo sacks, her friendship bracelets, her A-line floral-print dresses. Ray sold goat butter and the eggs we collected from the feathered bellies of hens. Carol sold canned tomatoes, peas, squash. Waterfall hand-dipped wicks into rainbow bee waxes and sold the candles in bundles.

My sister Halo took over the accounting as soon as she learned basic math. None of the adults thought it was strange, a kid managing the cash. She put together all the money that came in from the market and budgeted our spending. My sister was all straight lines; I felt curved and knotted beside her. She added and subtracted. I drew.

At night, Dado made secret objects to ward off evil. I hugged the backs of trees and watched him weld rebar into oval zeppelins with hanging stone eyes. He lassoed branches together in the shape of a star. He dusted every leaf of an oak with pure-powdered pigments we found, and let nature have her way with them.

Before the King Kennedys, Dado had tried to sell his sculptures. Rejection was like a torn-open wound in him. No gallery would ever take him. They'd never take him seriously. We talked about art, always, but he wouldn't talk about why the galleries had ignored his work.

Sculptures. You would never call them that. Was it because you couldn't sell them? Because they bled rust, because the gypsy moths made webs in them? Was it because they collected spiders and birds, because nobody saw them but us and the spooks who watched you from the trees?

He wanted to be known. He hated that he never was.

"Stay on the ground," he said. He'd grab my hand with his callused paw and pull me earthward. The musk of his hair overwhelmed me. "See the veins on this leaf, and how they match the veins in this ear?" He held a goat still and directed: "Follow the line of its head on that paper with that charcoal. See if you see it any differently."

He said the earth's heartbeat matched my own, and every day, when I woke up, I felt it.

Dado listened to WBAI, the renegade public radio station. The news, it would set him off, send him on these tangents. "The man, he's got to destroy his children to build his industry. Eat your young. Give guns to the kids to do your dirty work, that's right. It's all the big plan of the FBI—and don't think they don't see us. Oh, they're coming for us—like they did the Kennedys and King and Malcolm X. They've got a file on us. One day, they're going to bust us wide open."

Except he was the only one who could see them.

After the Vietnam War, Carter brought a few years of sanity until Reagan got elected. Dado said that the new president intended to sell the country to the rich. He started an underground newspaper called *Carter Lives!*, wrote long arti-

Who lit the match?

cles called "Against Ambition" and "Why Greed Kills," and handed it out at the market. He welded metal scarecrows and put them on the edges of the property to frighten the spooks watching him. After John Lennon got shot, he slipped into a place where no one could reach him. Not even Ma.

You thought the world was going to hell, the spooks were going to kill every good man left on earth, including you.

When Dado accused him of destroying his Lennon albums—which had actually been damaged by rain—Randy left with Carol. Krishna told us later he became a banker and bought a house in Larchmont.

There were thirteen of us left.

Then, at age fourteen, what Dado had declared the Age of Reason—the time in a person's life when they are to choose, or are given, a purpose—Halo broke free. She had been following the girls who wore satin jackets at the market. She made friends with them, the "Norms." She hid a Barbie doll in her bunk; I knew about it, even Ma did, but she let it go, like maybe she secretly hoped Halo would be a Norm, too, someday. The girls taught my sister about the world beyond the scarecrows. On her birthday, Halo called a family meeting in the mess area. Everyone was there.

She announced: "From now on, my name is Marilyn, and I want to go to public school."

We had never been to public school. The adults taught us—Jan had been a teacher. With all the work of the commune, and all we learned there, there was no room for school. I glanced at the other kids; we waited to hear what our parents would say.

Dado's husky-dog eyes started glowing with blue fury. He hadn't expected this. "No. You learn valuable, real lessons here. We teach you what you need to know."

Jan shook her head; beside her, Krishna shook his, like they'd already discussed it. Jan said slowly, "You know, Peter, I don't think it's a bad idea. Besides, Halo can choose her own purpose. We all agreed on that."

Halo was the oldest, the first.

She said, "I have the right to know things, aside from chicken shit."

Dado opened his mouth and this eerie choke came out. His fearful face got that *You're all against me* look. The point of his nose tilted down, his long wiry hair went electric. "Not you, Halo. None of those monkey rules for you."

"My name is Marilyn, like Monroe," Halo said. "And I'm going."

"You're my daughter and you're not changing your fucking name to Marilyn!" Dado raised his voice. "I won't have you destroyed by the system."

Waterfall's voice was soothing, like her name. "Hey, Peter? What's going on, man? Something's happening to you. You're getting really paranoid. We're worried about you." It was the first time anyone dared say it to him.

"You said I could decide for myself, Daddy," Marilyn said. She was crying by then. The rest of us kids huddled together. "You taught me that I could be anything, once I have my purpose. Well, I want to go to school. I want to be someone with a running toilet, a high-school diploma, a college education."

"A toilet!" Dado was shaking, that jittery shake of his leg that meant trouble. Then he shouted, "You want a fucking toilet?" He grabbed a ceramic mug and threw it. It smashed against the wall. Ma let out a cry and put her face in her hands. He said in a low voice, "You know the FBI has a file on us; they're learning our plans through a rat. Are you that rat, Halo?" He turned in a slow, menacing circle. "Are you, Ray? Maybe you, Hawk?"

No one could look at him after that.

Soon, Jan and Krishna split for good. Over the next few years, one by one, they all did.

Things went fallow. Dado stopped working the gardens, stopped keeping us in line. He set about stockpiling planks and nails. Ma took to knitting with a fury. She got in the pickup and drove to the city more often to buy her yards of fabric, making more clothes to sell, as if those clothes could get us out of the King Kennedys.

Marilyn went to school. I wanted to follow her, to see who she talked to and what she was up to, but I couldn't leave Dado. Even if he didn't seem to notice I was there.

I didn't take a single bath that whole year. I slept in trees. I smelled of goat grease and wore their skins after we ate them. Dado wouldn't touch the meat.

Last spring, he built that goddamn geodesic dome with everything he'd stockpiled, and I helped him. I loved the feel of a heavy hammer in my hand, the silver sound of it hitting a nail. Like we were getting somewhere, like maybe we would have a toilet someday. Soon as we got the first floor in, he tore down the yurt, and we took up residence. But he and Ma had stopped talking, and the space between them dried up like old leaves.

The day after the dome got done, he went and got a job at the chemical plant in Jersey. None of us asked him why. We didn't know what to say. It was like he had caved in, like any last bit of hope he had was gone. I wanted to kick my sister, shake my mother, tell them, "Do something! Help him!"

In the fall, I started leaving the King Kennedys, wandering around Staten Island, going into the city, because what

On the ferry, at the seaport, looking at the sailing ships and wishing I was on one of them headed to fucking Italy.

the fuck else was I going to do? Everyone was gone.

Blake and the fires came when Reagan proposed a planetary shield that would explode atomic bombs in space. The

Star Wars plan. It struck something deep in Dado—deep and screwed up and far, far away. He built eleven stone fire pits around the dome, a master number with an intense vibration that he believed would protect us. When he came home from work, he shucked down to his shorts, fired every pit, and danced while drumming and shouting wild poetry. Some nights, I danced with him; we danced like we could see a whole layer of the world nobody else saw. Because when your dado loses his mind, you might as well go with him.

Only he didn't take me all the way.

Sitting in the shelter with nothing left, I drew on that pile of paper what I could remember, like it would all disappear if I didn't.

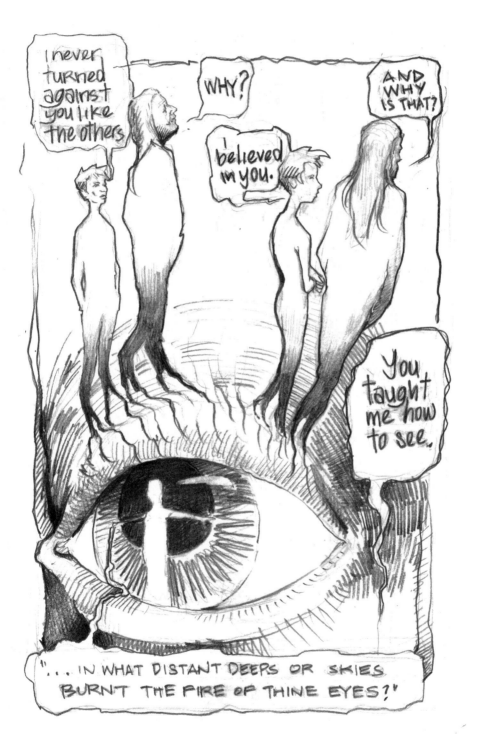

5

EVERY DAY FOR two weeks after the fire, I visited Miss Gray. I talked to her through paper, showed her all the stuff inside me. She gave me tests and advice, asked me if I thought it was my fault, what happened. *I should've helped him. I could've stopped him. Maybe if I danced harder, if Ma had . . . if Marilyn had . . . if we had . . .*

Then, Miss Gray called us all in and said, "We found you a place in the city."

"A place of our own?" I asked.

She smiled. "It's an SRO—a single-room-occupancy hotel—but it's got everything you need to get by."

We'd go late that afternoon, after Ma signed all the forms. April Fools' Day.

We took almost nothing with us. We had almost nothing.

On the subway, unless you were sitting down, bad breath

and bodies stumbled into you. That always made me long for air. I wasn't used to crowds; I hated being underground. Whenever I went to the city, I went only as far as I could walk, but I could walk miles. Now, I tried to make myself one with the subway car, one bee in a giant hive, like I used to at concerts in the park. But I wasn't feeling very Zen. I pressed my back into the door so nothing could sneak up behind me. Marilyn hung on to a pole, pretending she didn't know us. Ma sat with her hands folded in her lap, a shopping bag stuffed between her feet.

The handwriting caught my eyes. It was everywhere, like shouts from hidden mouths. Messages scribbled in ink on the ceilings, over ads, even on the maps. I tried to read them. Something about them reminded me—the drawings I used to do on walls when we went scavenging in empty factories and abandoned houses. I stared at their swoops and zags and sudden straight lines. I took out some paper and copied them.

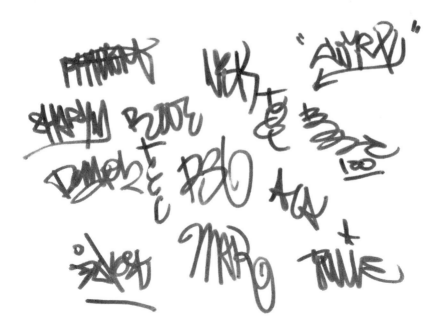

Beside me, scratched into the metal, was the word PRAY.

"Next stop," Marilyn said.

We bundled out, into the musty station. Up on the street, it smelled of pizza and cold concrete. Car horns blared, tires screeched, a police siren flashed, a fire truck thundered by. Brick and stone and mortar met my eyes everywhere I looked. It was worse than Brooklyn, trees puny and thin and very nearly dead. People hurried past me, brushing me with their arms. Twilight began, the shimmery night threat devouring day. Streetlights lit a newspaper stand covered in handwriting under a sign that said TE AMO. We stopped at an Italian deli where Ma bought American cheese and bologna, Wonder Bread, and a bottle of 7-Up, shit food like they served at the shelter. We passed a boarded-up building strapped with caution tape, scrawled with more writing—not much I could read except U82GOOD, PRINCE. I'd always written inside empty buildings with nobody watching. I tried to decipher these words like some coded message.

Our place was on 85th Street, a narrow building made of gray stone, with wide stairs and a curved metal fence painted black that held in a line of overflowing garbage cans, putrid even in the cold. A guy and a girl sat on the steps, cigs burning in their yellowed fingers. As we started up, they didn't look at us. They didn't look at each other either, their eyes stuck in the half distance.

Four dingy flights up, opposite the stairs, an unshaven

man reeking of booze slept on the floor outside a door marked TOILETS. Down a bit, Ma unlocked 418.

I didn't know what I was expecting—my own room? A bathroom? This was what Miss Gray meant by "hotel"?

A bunk bed stood by a small bay window that looked out onto the street. Next to it, a faded blue couch and two orange plastic chairs faced a television set on a milk crate. Opposite, an electric burner sat on a half fridge: our kitchen. A folding card table with four folding chairs stood for the dining room. After weeks on a cot with thirty other families, I drank in the privacy. At least that.

"This is hell," Marilyn said.

"It's temporary," Ma said.

I took the top bunk, claiming my space, and rested my head on the musty pillow. Dust tickled my nose; I sneezed. Ma turned on the TV.

In commercials, kids boogied down the street with a Coke in their hand; suburban dads drank Bud by the BBQ. They ate burgers. "Have it your way!" On shows, invisible people laughed at jokes. Streams of top-ten tips on how to get out stains floated by. Everyone was clean and smelled of green money. I couldn't stop watching. I imagined being one of them, then I felt sick. My pits stank, my hair was ragged and oily.

Marilyn braved the public showers to get washed for school. She put on a nightie, got in the bottom bunk for her

beauty rest. Ma took the couch. Neither of them mentioned that I was going to school myself, as if it were too weird, as if they had to see it to believe it, as if it might not happen at all. I crashed out in my clothes. Later, I woke to the gray light of the TV. Something crawled up the wall in front of me—a roach. The kids at the shelter smacked them dead by the dozens, taking pleasure in the instant death.

I pinched it off and held it in my hand, its legs tickling my palm. In the yurt, spiders and ants would creep in, warmed by the hard-packed dirt floors. We put bugs out like unwanted guests; here, I didn't know what to do with it.

Ma lay wide awake, staring at the screen. Little TVs reflected in her eyes, the action outside of her, nothing inside.

Footsteps paced above, a man snored below. I climbed down from the top bunk.

"Ma?"

"Hmmmmm?"

"Hey, Ma, I have to go to the bathroom, and it's, you know, the middle of the night," I said. Out in the hall, the guy still slept beside the bathroom. I could see him from the peephole. Marilyn must've stepped right over him.

"I'll listen for you," Ma said.

Listen for what? My screams as he grabbed my legs and pulled me down?

Ma cut off to start our life over. *Don't look back* was the thing that kept her going forward. I saw what it cost her. She said people in the city didn't care anymore—they had nothing to lose. That's how I felt: *nothing to lose.*

Did nothing to lose mean you had everything to gain?

I brought my white Swiss Army knife with the screwdriver and awl, two blue ballpoint pens, and my drawing book out with me; my bandage had come off, and now the only time I felt safe was inside my black watch cap and coat. In the hall, I let the roach loose and didn't use the bathroom. I went out to the stoop, into the fake city light, starless and bitter cold. Everything hard-edged, gum-stuck, broken-glass.

Looking at my blank page, I didn't even know where to begin.

I drew Dado burning, flames coming from his head, and I swore I could feel him pouring from my veins. His head had been on fire for years. That's what crazy was like.

I sat on the freezing stoop, but it felt like the drawing was burning a hole right through my thighs. I tore it out carefully, balled it, and tossed it on the ground. I drew it again, like I needed to get him right—his face, I kept getting the wrong face. The wrong nose, wrong eyes. Fire Pop, burned by the secret agents inside his own mind.

I tore pages out, digging for him. There was nothing left of him after the fire, they told us—not even bones. I couldn't stand to sit in the cold, couldn't stand the pricks in my own heart, the sense that I was truly dead. I got up and walked a few blocks to a park. Central Park. Skeleton trees jabbed at my insides. I dragged my nails across their bark. Yellow cabs sharked by.

On top of the stone wall, I sat and drew him. I tore and threw him, like I was spreading his ashes.

He brought me a roll of paper that night. What if I had stopped him? Made him talk to me a little longer? Thinking of him made me want to tear the stuffing from my heart, just tear it out and not feel it anymore. No, I didn't feel anything, that was the truth. If I took my knife and nicked at my wrists like those shelter girls, I wouldn't feel it, not one bit. I could hit a vein and watch the blood come pouring out, use its redness to paint on the cold ground.

I was walking around completely stripped of my life, hair singed, homeless as a stray, half my ear gone. Half an orphan.

Tomorrow, I was going to start school. School. Me in school, me and school. Those things just didn't seem to go together.

No wonder I couldn't sleep.

6

THE DIFFERENCE BETWEEN Staten Island and Manhattan was the difference between circles and squares. Manhattan had blocks. Angles, straight lines. Nothing soft, like leaves or dirt, nothing to sink your fingers into unless you wanted to hit dog shit.

School was on the block next to the housing project. On our way there, Marilyn cornered me with a jade-green velvet band: "Here, let me tie this around your head. You'll look so much better." I knew she didn't want to be seen with me, though she wouldn't say as much. I pulled my watch cap down and wouldn't let her touch me. I was on my own. I didn't want to go along with this, but the government made me do it. In my new black back-pack were the spiral notebook, flimsy airmail pad, and brown fine-point pen Ma had given me with the words "These will

bring you luck." After everything, she still believed in mojo.

As we walked together, Marilyn and I, suits and skirts smelling of cologne and soap rushed toward the subway. Homeless men with plastic-bag feet slept on traffic island benches. I kept trying to swallow the marble stuck in my throat. When we got to Cady Public High School, we stood outside closed doors in the rectangular block of dirty white brick where I'd be stuck all day. Kids slapped hands and tried to trip each other. I had spent my life free, and the whole idea of school unnerved me. It just sucked. Especially with a torn ear and chick-fuzz hair that still itched. Down my back trickled this fear someone would pull off my cap and leave me naked. I pushed down the urge to run as fast as I could as far as I could away from this flock of freaks.

But nobody was looking at me. Boys stared at Marilyn, all cool in her heels and navy peacoat; even her bandaged hand looked crisp and white. I stood darkened by her gleam, taking

advantage of her shadow to observe. Black kids, white kids,
Puerto Ricans, everybody kaleidoscoping into their own
groups. I didn't care; I didn't need anyone.

We went inside and looked for the office. The khaki walls
cracked under years of paint. Written up the mustard-and-
ketchup staircases were scrawls I couldn't read. But the words
along the hallway spoke to me.

Question everything, they said, and below it, *Why?*

ME ONE, and, next to that, *me too.*

Down a bit: *Pete was here and now he's gone, he left his name to carry on, those who knew him knew him well, those who didn't can go to hell.*

Loudmouthed kids jostled into me and didn't notice, the ceilings were water stained, the halls stank of rotting food— was this what all those tests were for? Miss Gray talked me into it: *Soon as we apply for emergency public assistance, they're going to want you in school. Take the tests, do it for your family, you'll be fine.* Marilyn had already applied to colleges.

An elbow banged into me, knocking my bag to the floor. I pulled my cap down over my forehead as I picked it up.

The lady in the office read over my tests and put me in sophomore year. She took one look at the ballpoint blueprint drawings all over my hands, and she put me in art class two days a week.

Nobody had tested me on that.

7

SOMEHOW, I MADE it through that first labyrinthian day
of hallways and faces and questions. The next day, the art
teacher, Mr. Garci, made the biggest fuss over me being
new, but I didn't hear a word he said because I was staring
at the room.

There were jars and jars of paints—red like strawberries,
blue like lollipops that leave a stain on your mouth, green as
a field of mint, yellow like lemons, purple as grapes broken
off the vine, spheres fresh and wet in your hand. Against the
wall stood stretched canvases. Were they for us? Over there,
a shelf of paper—big paper, small paper—next to markers
lined up in neatly chromatic rows. What did a person learn
here? Did they let you do whatever you wanted? A wild cry of
surprised joy strained at my throat. Doors flung open in my

head—I wanted to eat paint, let it zing out my fingers, get lost in the colors in this room.

Felt like I'd been waiting to breathe. Here was air.

Kids sat at worktables cratered with the knives and pens of kids who came before. On one was written: ALL YOUR DREAMS BELONG TO US.

Everyone had a thing out in front of them—like they were each building something from cardboard.

Mr. Garci stopped them. As my eyes roamed the faces, I felt like the new polar bear in the zoo. One of those ratty, self-destructive polar bears who rub holes in their white coats, looking at all the other animals in their cages.

"Our class is a place of imagination and safety," Mr. Garci told me. "You're welcome here as long as you respect the creativity of others and you don't cut off a finger, yours or anyone else's."

I saw some curious faces, interesting faces, even some beautiful faces, though I couldn't focus on any particular person. Most were like they just wanted to get back to work.

"Why don't you tell us something about yourself, Aurora?" Mr. Garci asked.

That question again. What could I tell them about Dado, the house burning down, him trying to take us with him? I pulled my coat tighter around me.

"People call me Ror. I'm from Staten Island," I said too fast. Judgment shimmered over the faces.

"And why did you decide to take art class?"

I blinked at the kids, thinking, *The lady put me here*, thinking, *Drawing is the only way I can explain anything, and somehow, she knew that.*

"You the rebel of the family?" I shot a look at the teacher, in jeans and a tie-dyed shirt, his long blond hair pulled into a ponytail, his open face smiling at me. He looked like a fake-o hippie. What did he know about rebels?

When I didn't answer, he said to the class: "Okay, folks, I'm going to charge everyone here with helping Ror find her way in this classroom, is that a deal?" A couple of them looked the way I felt—like I was reading a Grimm fairy tale with the good pages glued shut. "Who wants to volunteer to explain our project to Ror?"

A long, thin boy in a black leather cap raised his finger. I met his eyes. Cool, stone, Smokey. He didn't look away, and I felt stupidly grateful.

"You got it, Trey." The kids went back to work as Mr. Garci made room for me at the table beside the boy.

"'Sup," he said. He gave me a cardboard box and scissors. "You cold or somethin'?"

My numb heart longed to talk, but I didn't want to tell him my whole sad story. I stared at the cardboard and pulled my coat closer around myself. "I may need to run outside real quick," I managed.

"Ain't no fire drills since I been to this school, if that's what you're thinkin'," he said.

I glanced at him quickly. "What, fire?"

He held his hands up. "Yo, I was gonna say keep chill, but you already cold as ice."

I found I couldn't stop looking at his face. His caramel eyes were like an echo, an open cave. I tried lifting my lips into a smile, but I was out of practice. He grinned and shook his head and got back to work.

I slipped off my coat and hung it on the chair.

I looked at his box.

"We're playing architect," he said. "Garci says to imagine and build the house we want to live in someday."

The dome. I'd already built it.

"You know, a real house, not no roach holes like we live in."

Dado destroyed it.

I looked around—most of the kids had cut rectangles for the door and squares for the windows. Some taped two together to make a skyscraper, or left the box intact and marked it up. Dado and I had built a geodesic dome. I picked up the scissors and started trying to cut through the cardboard, but it was too thick. I took out my Swiss Army knife.

"Girl, you crazy? Garci'll bust you, he sees that," Trey said.

A triangle is twice as strong
as a Rectangle.
— B. Fuller

In four cuts, I had the thing apart. I slit the rest of the box into slats: the struts for the triangles. Next thing I knew, everybody was quiet, looking at me. I kept my head down and my hands busy. I notched the ends and fitted the pieces together into a circle. I built until Mr. Garci told us to clean up. Which I did. I put my dome on the shelf full of other houses and left the room when the bell rang, before that Trey guy could say anything more to me.

BY THE END of that first week, I felt like I had a sign stuck on my back, one that glowed: DO NOT APPROACH. I came home to find Ma at the table, brushing out this brown-and-blonde wig while Marilyn sat on the couch, her books spread on the floor, her hair sprayed big and tied with a pink-and-gray ribbon, her wrists ringed with black rubber bracelets. I felt a weird vibe. They were up to something.

"Ror, I got this for you," Ma said. I threw my keys onto the table and walked around her, not sure what to expect. With frantic purpose, she spent her days knitting and tying knots into every bit of yarn she could find, like her creations would fix us somehow, if only she worked fast enough. Today, she wore a new smock she'd sewn by hand. It fit her wrong. Was she gaining weight? She seemed sick and strange. She'd had some job interview to teach something at the YMCA, but she wouldn't get it looking like that.

"Me? A wig?" I asked, looking at my sister. "Whose idea might that be?"

"Not mine. I think you need some decent shoes," Marilyn said, "not those shitkickers."

"My social worker said the wig would help you with your identity," Ma said, spinning the thing around with a frown of doubt. "I don't know if that's true."

Maybe before, I would have let them make clothes for me, or change the way I looked. But we were here now. I took off my cap and ran my fingers up the back of my short hair. I had snipped off the ragged edges. The itch was starting to go away. "What's wrong with my identity?" I asked.

"I told Ma how I heard kids talking in school. They think you're a psychopath," Marilyn said. Was that why no one spoke to me? Was it the knife?

"I'm not wearing any wig," I said.

"Come on. You'll be like Andy," Marilyn said. Now I knew it was really her idea. She loved Andy Warhol because he hung out with Halston and Bianca Jagger. Andy wore a platinum wig—he used it to change himself, to become someone else. I loved him for all his off-centered prints, the way he went outside the lines. I took the wig from the table and looked at it. "It'll soften you up," Marilyn added.

"I worry you don't feel womanly, Ror," Ma said.

What the hell? At seventeen, did I need to feel *womanly*? Why would I *ever* in my fucking *life* need to feel womanly?

I put the thing on my head anyway and looked in the mirror. Awful. Marilyn sighed, came over, and switched it around. I'd had it on backward. Better. Much better. I even looked kind of sexy.

"You look like a girl again," Ma said.

"Maybe you'll stop acting like a burn victim," Marilyn said.

"I *am* a burn victim," I said.

"Ror, please, it was only a minor burn. Hair takes time to grow," said Ma.

But all that grew was this chick fuzz, only my bangs still long in front.

"I broke my fingers falling out that window. You don't see me acting psycho." Marilyn held up the bandaged left hand that she carefully wrapped in clean gauze every day.

"Just because I'm not a slave to fashion doesn't mean I'm psycho."

"You do need to spruce up your wardrobe, Ror," Ma said, tapping her chin with a finger. "I wish I had my sewing machine. Marilyn, help me; what can we do here?"

My sister was the Dime Store Fashion Maven. She could come out of Woolworth's with cheap accessories and make them look like a million bucks, or at least a hundred. Me, I could wrap pearls around my neck and still look like a swine. The way I used markers and pen, my hands were never clean. In my brain, it wasn't a contest—staying clean and pretty, or drawing something on paper, on my hands, my arms, my pants.

I stood up straight in the mirror and poofed out the fake bangs. I'd rather Ma got me a rainbow wig, long and straight to my waist. I just couldn't see myself in this brown-blonde mess seriously walking into that high school. I could already hear the whispers behind my back—*What is it, Halloween?*— *What is she supposed to be? Oh my God, ha, ha, ha!*

Since when did I ever care what other people thought?

I did. I cared. Shit, everybody cared unless you were blind or dumb, and even people like that cared. I was just really good at stuffing the care down inside me, swallowing it and digesting it and spitting it out.

I cared what Dado thought, and he was gone, and now I didn't know what to care about.

Rich people take everything for themselves. We all know that. Question is: Why can't anyone make them give it back?

My sister came over with a shoe box of beads and lace; she sorted out a headband and pushed it down around the wig.

"There," she said.

I looked into the mirror. I looked like I belonged in that movie *Hair*. Like some TV hippie. I pulled the headband thing down around my neck, flipped the wig sideways, and bared my teeth. Now I looked like I was in a band with Sid Vicious.

"Does this make me seem less of a psychopath?" I laughed.

They didn't answer.

I took off the wig and choker, ignoring their disappointed faces. "Ma, Marilyn, I appreciate your thoughtful efforts, but no thanks." I left the stuff on the table and got to drawing.

THE ONLY THING I ever wanted was to make pictures. I drew on the palms of my hands and the tops of my feet. I drew on other people, on walls, on desks, on tables. On paper. I made album covers for Jimi Hendrix, the Wailers, the Stones, the Ramones. I was the commune artist: I painted the sign for the King Kennedys, designed labels for the stuff we sold in the market, copied patterns for clothes.

I drew like people breathed.

I drew because if I didn't, I'd die.

I drew to follow the shape of the world, so I could understand how it worked and why I was here.

All right, fine, I drew because it made other kids like me—kids in parks where I hung out, kids I met on the ferry, at the seaport, at Clove Lakes, at Clay Pit Pond. Norm kids from Marilyn's school. I was the last King Kennedys holdout, and my drawings made Norms see me different—not just a long-hair from a squat, but a girl who had something. I drew Pinkie Parmigiana and the Bad Barbies, and my sister sold them to her Norm friends.

Bad Barbie: She's fifteen feet tall and can fit you in her pocket, smother you with her love. Bad Barbie: She eats ten boxes of donuts every night. Bad Barbie: She lets her hair get knotty and pigeons roost in it.

Pinkie Parmigiana was this punk girl in our comic *Peepull.* She lived in a radical commune with peepull and was always getting into trouble with them: "Pinkie blunders into a love triangle with Jeff and Ken. Oh, what a sticky mess!" or "Pinkie and her sister Blondie stumble on a dead body in the forest and bury it instead of calling the pigs. Pinkie can never sleep again."

Marilyn did the words.

We mimeographed the comix, and Marilyn sold them at her school for a quarter each. They were a hot seller; we made loads. We split the profits and bought forbidden salami and packaged cheese. I bought Snickers I ate in private. How many times did we break Number 7, the hardest one of all? 7. *No sugar, no meat. They just ain't good for you.*

I lost it all. All the stuff I drew, all my books.

At the Cady school library, I tried to find copies of the books Dado gave me. There was this great one of interviews

with my second favorite artist, Francis Bacon, who painted these freaky interiors with haunted faces and skeletal bodies. And another on the Mexican painter Frida Kahlo and her husband, Diego Rivera, who looked like a fat frog but painted like a prince. On my own, I'd secretly collected Andy Warhol scraps and bits and cutouts from the newspapers. Those, all of those, were gone.

Dado hated Warhol—said he was too busy trying to be a celebrity to make real art. He said real art was meant to be revolutionary, to overthrow oppressive powers—*Look at Diego Rivera's murals of Zapata. A farmer who became a hero to his people—that deserves a painting.* He loved sculptors like Rodin and Brancusi. To him, they were the real deal.

I thought Andy was the most real it could get. It was issue 3 of *Aspen Magazine* that got me started on him. I found it on a dusty shelf in an abandoned warehouse we were scavenging. Actually, at first, I thought it was a box of Fab laundry detergent. When I opened it, inside was all this *stuff*—a newspaper Andy called the *Plastic Exploding Inevitable* with a collage of comix on the cover, a flip book of a movie called *Buzzards Over Bagdad*, a collection of Pop Art postcards, a floppy LP of a guy from the Velvet Underground, and a trip ticket book about acid with a question: "Does LSD in sugar cubes spoil the taste of coffee?" I was like, *Shit! You can do this? You can make stuff like this and it's art?* I hid it under my sweater and took it home.

I looked through that box over and over, studying every bit of it, wondering who the heck this guy was—Andy Warhol, mastermind inside a Silver Dream Factory making everything Fab. That wasn't like anything Dado had taught me. I listened to the music of his art and fell in love. From then on, I followed Andy in the *Village Voice*, the *SoHo News*, whatever

I could get my hands on. Last year, I even took the ferry and walked all the way to this club in the city to find him, but none of the faces was his. I felt like a stupid groupie and never did that again.

Now that Dado was gone, my love for Andy seemed silly and small.

Walking home down Broadway, I caught my reflection in store windows, surprised like I was glancing at another girl, a tougher one, only to realize it was me. The self in the window glass hunched like a singed, beaten animal.

Right before the fire, I had decided that I didn't want to be a hippie anymore, so I grabbed hold of my long hair and cut it off at my neck.

I tried to remember who I was.

My identity.

But without Dado, without my drawings, my books, my collections, I had nothing to hold on to.

I reached the hotel and sat on the sunny stoop, drawing. I heard a voice say, "Yo, Staten Island, you followin' me?" and saw Trey coming up the steps, wearing a Sherlock Holmes–looking hat and carrying a sleeping little kid. A switch flicked on—*He lives here, and he's the only one in school who talks to me*—and some gladness flooded me. Some warmth. I stood up quickly, then sat down again, wondering if I should show him my drawing, or talk to him about art class. A sad-faced, pretty woman with his color eyes was behind him. She opened the

door, and he leaned against it while she went upstairs with the groceries. He waited for me to answer, hiking up the little kid, a cool smile playing on his face.

I said, "Hey. Yeah. I mean, no."

"Don't tell me you *live* in this dump?"

I nodded. "418."

"No shit! I'm in 621," he said. "Lemme tell you, don't trust the dude in 534, no matter what he says. And make sure you stuff Brillo under the radiator, or you gonna have a pizza party with them mice comin' in."

"What about the drunk guy who sleeps in the hall?"

"Watch how you talk about my uncle." His eyes laughed. "Just playin'. Joe won't do you no harm." He smiled at me, adjusted the kid's legs around his hips, and went inside.

I felt it then, the emptiness. How was it you could be so alone in a city of millions?

10

IN ART CLASS the next week, Trey threw his sketchbook on the desk and sat beside me. "'Sup, Staten Island."

We'd worked on our projects side by side but hadn't really talked. On the cover of his book, I noticed the writing like I'd seen in the subway and on the walls, only his was good, and in color, and I wanted to ask him what it was, how he'd done it, but I couldn't find the words.

"'Sup," I said back.

We met eyes, and I studied his, today the musky brown-green of fern moss. He tilted his green fedora down and eased back into his chair until I couldn't see him anymore. But I had the image of him imprinted in my mind.

Garci handed out paper and asked us to draw the still life with a blue bottle he'd set up on his desk. I'd done a million of these—the round bowl, the flat dish. Trey had the same sharp eyes I'd seen in pictures of Stokely Carmichael. I drew the way his tight curls burst out from under the brim of his hat, his rounded features—that curved nose—was he part Cherokee? His lips were square at the top, so full at the bottom.

"Hey there, I see you've found something more interesting to do."

I looked up; Mr. Garci was inspecting my work. I was supposed to draw the bottle. I reached for fresh paper.

"No, no, let's see what you've got there," he said, moving my hand away. I couldn't tell if he was smiling, or angry that I didn't do the assignment. "You seem to have some experience in this."

"I just—"

"No, it's good, Ror, but it's a little flat. If you want to add some depth, see if you can focus on what's going on *behind* Trey's face," Mr. Garci said.

Flat?

"What?" Trey said. "You drawin' me?" He looked over and his face changed. Soured, darkened, like I had drawn an insult. His head snapped back, and he pushed his hand out as if to brush me off. "Yo, I don't look like that! Why you make my eyes so small?"

Small?

Everyone turned to look, and I held myself steady. What were they going to say? Would I hear more of these insults, or would someone understand it?

Mr. Garci said, "Okay, folks, art is not a spectator sport. I want to see those still lifes done by the end of class."

Trey's eyes narrowed. "You think you draw good—I'm gonna draw you—see how you like that."

"But I didn't mean it that way."

"And you two—" Mr. Garci said.

Trey held up his hand. "Nah, nah, I'm gonna get this one, Mr. G. I'm gonna show her who can do it better." He made a big drama, turning his chair around to face me. He grabbed fresh paper and started drawing me.

"It's not a competition. Let's just see what you two can do," Mr. Garci said as he drifted down the row.

Trey drew fiercely. What was he looking at? Drawing, I'd always been in the driver's seat. Was this what it felt like to be drawn? The precision of laser beams, his intense eyes, like he could slice a design into me. Would he make me look like a psychopath? There was nowhere to hide. His eyes pinned me down.

I could tell by his hand motions that he was using crosshatch and shading. He worked fast, his other hand holding the paper away from me. He was so focused, like he wanted to win, like it was a game, who could be better, faster.

He slapped his drawing down next to mine, and said, "There. That's how it's done."

I felt myself gasp—*wow*. Like looking at me, only a deeper me, a better me. How had he gotten me so clearly, so fast, and with so few lines?

Our drawings were so different. Garci came around to compare. "Good. These are good rough sketches. You two have distinct styles."

"You damn right, I got style," Trey said. "I got *miles* of style."

The class laughed; now everyone was paying attention.

"But Ror, what's the matter with Trey's drawing?"

"He drew me too pretty," I said too fast. Titters broke out behind me.

Mr. Garci said, "That wasn't what I was thinking. Trey, what's the unusual point of interest in Ror's face?"

"The unusual?" Trey was serious, studying the surface of me.

"What attracts your eye?"

Trey stared, his look crawling over my skin. I touched my ear. "She's got them circles."

Circles?

"These circles here?" Mr. Garci said, drawing with a finger in the air around my eyes. "Okay, what do they mean? Explore that in your sketch next time."

Was my nightmare life so easy to read?

"And, you, Ror, don't gloss over Trey's flaws. Where is this scar, and this?"

Trey pushed Mr. Garci's hand away. "What you talkin' 'bout, Mr. G? I ain't got no flaws!" Laughter.

The bell rang. Everybody jumped from their seats, including Trey.

"Next time," Mr. Garci said to me, "focus on pulling out his personality."

As he left, Trey didn't look back at me.

Next time.

I followed him out of the room.

11

I WANTED TO ask Trey where he learned to draw like that. As I neared him in the hallway, a couple of guys went over and slapped hands with him. I forced myself on, until I was standing right in front of him, watching him joke with his buddies.

I said, "Trey, hey, Trey, your drawing was—"

He turned, his eyes triumphant, and said, "That's right, Staten Island, you know I beat your ass."

I felt my cheeks burn. "*What?*"

He said, "I beat you so bad, you ain't never gonna come up for air."

His friends cracked up. "Yo, you beat her?"

The one with long hair said, "'Staten Island'?"

"Ain't that where cows live or somethin'?" a Chinese kid went. "Moo."

"Nah, ain't nothing on Staten Island but garbage." This from a little pimply boy.

I felt for my knife in my pocket.

Trey said, "I beat you so bad, the vultures gonna come pick at your old drawing."

"Fuck you," I said.

His face changed, taken aback. "Ooh," the boys jeered.

Then he smirked, "You wish you could, Staten Island."

I backed off, their laughter ringing in my ears.

"We's just messin' with you," Trey said, but I was already hurrying away.

How did that go so wrong? I walked home alone, my eyes

burning hot, even in the cold wind. The monstrous buildings made faces, groups of girls turned from me in horror, one of them laughed at me, her mouth dripping red. I kept thinking of his words—*I beat you.* I beat you. Nobody had ever beat me—nobody even saw it that way!

I was grateful no one was home when I got in. I switched on the TV and took out my schoolbooks and tried to concentrate, but my eyes kept drifting back to the Afterschool Special, some sappy Wonder Bread love story. I must've fallen asleep, because something woke me. Dancing in the hall: *Badum bum, badum bum. Badum badum, bum bum.* I looked out the peephole and saw it was Trey, jumping down the stairs to some rhythm in his head.

I grabbed my coat and got outside just in time to see him cross Columbus Avenue. I followed him for another block west on 85th, keeping a half block between us. Then, I saw him stop. I ducked behind a parked car. I didn't know what I'd say to him if I caught up.

He looked around and went into a weedy lot. I hurried and saw him disappear in the dark of night around the back of an old brownstone, the one with the front door chained shut. The lot was seeded with dumped garbage bags, used condoms, cigarette butts, beer cans.

Was he scavenging?

I walked away, down the block, around the corner, trying to talk myself into shadowing him inside.

I went into abandoned buildings all the time, so what was stopping me now?

By the time I got back there, I'd talked myself into it. Dammit, I'd done this before. I could handle Trey alone.

I glanced up and down the street, then went into the lot and found a way to slip inside through the loose basement door. The floors were strewn with empty wine bottles, tinfoil, needles. I looked at the stuff, wondering what a shot of heroin would feel like. Not that I was into drugs. The couple of times I smoked pot, I got real paranoid. Pot could make some people fly, but not me.

Upstairs, a streetlight shone through the window, picking up the neglected beauty of the room—a fireplace with a marble mantel. Carved moldings around wooden doors. I imagined Dado prying off this stuff, piling it up, taking it home and putting it to good use. Now there was no use.

I stopped and listened upstairs for junkies or drunks, but even they had deserted this place. Trey wasn't making a sound. Handwriting lined the walls like I noticed everywhere in the city now, like a massive snarl of roots, spies talking to each other. Glass crunched under my boots as I climbed another flight of steps.

On this floor, a bathtub with lion's feet, a broken-down cabinet.

I went higher, to the third floor, marveling at the old paper peeling gracefully from the walls. On the fourth, I heard rumbling, laughter, moving around. More voices than one.

Shit. He *wasn't* alone.

I backed down the stairs, wishing there wasn't so much broken glass. A door slammed above me, and feet went running down the hall. I skittered into a nearby room, praying they'd leave without spotting me. I stared through a crack in the door and held my breath. Laughter, the feet tramping down the stairs. When they got to my level, I saw Trey with the other boys from school.

I held my breath to disappear as they ran by.

What were they doing here?

I waited for silence. Then I stepped into the hall and hurried upstairs, following a bitter smell into the room where they'd been hanging out. As soon as I pushed the door open, it struck me.

A painting. The biggest painting I'd ever seen in real life. Bigger even than ones in the museum.

Covering the entire wall, up to the high ceiling, the colors and huge shapes in code. I'd caught glimpses of them on the subway cars, but not like this. Not in a *room*. It filled the space; it seemed to belong just right here, to transform this forgotten place into a secret marvel. I moved closer to study it in the pumpkin-flesh streetlight. Looked like Trey had been working on it a long time. The paint was so smooth and flat, the lines so crisp and even. The colors were as perfectly blended as the *Dark Side of the Moon* album.

How did he—how did he do it?

I saw, then. He knew something I didn't know.

I stood and stared, feelings flooding me—the way it vibrated off the wall, as if it was alive and singing—the blood surged back into my veins, the vacant lot of my heart filled with pumping red that made me want to live, to find colors, to do *that*.

On the floor were cans of paint, spray paint. *Spray paint! That was it!* I picked up a can. What would happen if I pressed the button? I tried it. It sputtered and sprayed only air. I dug through the cans hungrily, wanting to make it work. I pressed one button after another, until I found one that shot out paint with a kick like a gun. I took it to the wall—a burst of black. Oh! The power! I shaped it, trying to stay up with it, the quickness of the spray. This was the stuff! I wanted more, I had to ask Trey—

Trey.

I stumbled back from the wall and saw with horror I had sprayed the black on the painting. I had sprayed out a Fire Pop.

A Fire Pop.

It was quick and it was right, the best I'd ever done, but why had I sprayed that? The can burned into my hand as if it wanted me to throw it back. Instead, I shoved it in my coat pocket, flew down the stairs, and out into the street.

12

IN MY TOP BUNK, I held that can close, slipping the metal ball around and around. Beneath my subterranean layers, I felt the power of spray and knew I needed to get more, to learn how to use it. Sounds of that painting sang in me, colors swam in my head like schools of exotic fish flashing by.

That black Fire Pop like a mark on my soul.

"What's that sound?" Marilyn whispered from below, her voice thick with sleep.

I stopped. "Nothing."

"It's something. Tell me what."

We'd shared secrets, broken the deepest Manifesto laws together. But I didn't want to tell her about Trey, the building, the painting. That was mine. "It's just some junk I found," I said lightly.

Our mother slept with her back to us, tucked on the couch.

"Let me see," Marilyn said. "Rora, let me see. Come on!" She was awake now. There was no hiding from her once she figured out that something was important to me. I leaned over the bunk and gave her the can. Reruns of *Family Feud* played on the TV, the gray reflecting on Marilyn's face as she put it together.

Spray paint = Graffiti.

"Where'd you find it?" she asked.

I told her about the abandoned building but not about the painting or Trey. She stared down at the can for a long time.

She lifted her head, finally, met my eyes. "You still doing that kid stuff?"

The insult stung.

"Give me a break, Rora. Don't go digging in other people's shit. We're trying not to be squatters anymore. You can do better than this. You can." She tossed the can back up onto my bed. "Grow up, little sister."

I listened to her settle. It flitted through my mind: *Maybe I could ask her for money,* but she'd never *give* me money for no reason—she hated when I asked her for anything unless I proved its necessity. *You can do better. I can't, you can.* From a book we read as kids.

The can in my fingers set my mind free—that wall must've been higher than twelve feet and wider than twenty; I had

never painted anything
so big. I wanted to know how
Trey made the colors do that, how he
reached the ceiling, what it felt like to
paint in that space—I could taste it, the
bitter smell of paint. I slipped out my notebook and
drew what I would do if I got myself some.

13

I RIFLED THROUGH Ma's purse and came up with a crumpled dollar, two dimes, and a handful of food stamps. I kept the money and left the stamps. I had no idea how much a can cost, or where to buy one, so I went hunting, up Broadway, past cheese stores and blue-haired ladies, bodegas and domino players, a movie theater playing *La Dolce Vita*, a boutique with busted glass.

Up on 92nd, I found this store, Jon's A#1 Art Supplies & Framing. The place took up half a block. Inside smelled of fresh-cut wood. I picked up pencils, pens, markers, brushes. I ran my fingers over sketchpads of creamy paper, squeezed tubes of yellow ochre and aquamarine blue and cadmium red, wishing it was all mine.

All the time, I looked for spray. I could practically taste it in my mouth like hard metal, that can, the feel of it in my hand, the kick, like starting up a chain saw.

The cover of a magazine stopped me: the mouth-pink screaming face of a Francis Bacon. I saw three Francis Bacon oil paintings together once at the Standish Museum with Dado. I stood in front of the triptych for an hour. It wasn't in a book. It was on the wall. Right in front of me. For real. I couldn't tear myself away from those smears of desperation. The way they shook.

A good painting is one that makes you gasp inside.

"You looking for something?" An old guy behind the counter picked at his teeth with a paper clip. I lifted my head, and there I saw, in perfect geometrical patterns, color-coded shelves of spray paint behind the counter.

"Um, yeah," I said. "How much is a can of that spray paint?"

He squinted his eyes at me. "What do you want with that stuff? What're you gonna do with it?"

I rubbed my mouth and looked down at my filthy hand. I felt my face smudged with ink from drawing and tried to wipe it off on my coat. It suddenly occurred to me: *graffiti might be illegal*.

He said, "What are you, an artist or a hoodlum?" What was he going on about? What did he care? "What you got in that book?" he asked.

I hugged the pad to my chest. "Nothing," I said.

"Let's see nothin'," he said.

His challenge did something to me. Like Trey. I didn't want to be whipped. His wrinkled hands with road-map-blue veins opened to me. I went up and put my worn-out drawing pad carefully on the counter. He flipped through the pages, then he looked up.

What was he thinking?

"You got a lot of good stuff here, kid," he said, his voice quieter. "What's your name?"

"Aurora. People call me Ror."

"Roar? Like a lion?" He smiled; I didn't. "Just a joke. I'm Jonathan. You could really do something with these, Ror. You got any more?"

"I lost—I lost a bunch of things," I said.

Jonathan reached under the counter and pulled out a new sketchpad and a pencil, thick like a stick of charcoal. "Take these," he said. "You don't need no can of spray paint. Trust me."

I stared. I didn't take handouts.

"It's a gift. Consider it a contribution from a fan," he said.

Warmth pressed down hard in the palm of my hand as I held the pencil. I took the pad warily, watching his eyes. He said, "Come back, when you done some more work, come back and show me." He was giving it to me. For keeps. What could I give him in return?

14

SCHOOL WAS THE last place to find space or privacy. Girls with braces bunched together, boys with pimples snapped bras and laughed maniacally, smooth kids in tight jeans and suede sneakers crowded on the steps with their boom boxes and skateboards, punks clung to the gated windows and smoked. Kids messed around in the dark staircases, smoking pot, making out. I'd already read all the books for English class, I lost the text for Spanish, and I stuck holes in everything with the pin on my compass.

Everywhere, I saw the writing like from the abandoned building. Did Trey do it? But there were distinct inks, assorted handwritings—so it was lots of kids who wrote on the walls. I glanced in notebooks and got glares back. *What you lookin' at?* How could I ask them what I wanted to know? *Are you one of them?*

In my coat pocket, I carried the spray can like a talisman.
I rehearsed it in my head—what I'd say when I got up my
nerve in art class. I'd take it out, say, "Trey, you know anything about this?"

Wait, no, that was dumb. I wouldn't say anything about
the can at all. Just the painting. No, I wouldn't say anything
about that either; I'd wait for him to talk. But he wouldn't
talk, because we had a fight over that drawing. Why had I
even drawn him in the first place?

Trey took his seat beside me and rubbed his forehead with
both hands and sighed heavy. His leg bounced furiously un-

der the table as we listened to Mr. Garci talk about this field trip we'd be taking to the Con-Mod Art Museum in May, something about getting permission slips signed.

I'd wrapped the spray can in cloth so no one would hear the *click click* it made when I walked. I thought maybe I'd tell him how great I thought the painting was, and we could be friends. He could teach me how to do it.

The way his leg bounced, I couldn't open my mouth.

"Okay, folks, let's get back to our still lifes. Those bottles aren't going to break no matter how much you draw them, so get to work," Mr. Garci said.

I took out my new sketchbook. It fell open to a Fire Pop. Trey's leg stopped moving. I closed the book real quick. Had he seen it? I tried to control my heartbeat, the wild thrill inside me that I had done something illegal on something that might be his.

I chanced a peek at him; now he was glaring at me.

I jutted my chin. "'Sup? You look like you're gonna explode," I said.

"Yeah," he said. "I got a score to settle."

"Oh, yeah? What happened?" I asked.

"Somebody went over my painting," he growled.

A stab of fear iced me. That was like a week ago. "What painting?"

"Never mind. I find out who it is, I'ma cut 'em up."

Is that the way he got that scar? I thought.

Mr. Garci came over. "Oh, you two going to draw each other again?"

Trey said, "Yo, Mr. G, I got her the first time. Don't need to do her again."

"Come on, Trey. You know the perfection of art is in its repetition," Garci said.

"Repetition! You know how many throw-ups I done?"

"I'm not talking about your Neanderthal markings. You know what I think of that."

"Yeah, yeah, I heard it," Trey muttered.

Garci said, "This time, why don't you focus on her eyes?"

I looked into Trey's face, and he stared back. Tension strung his body tight. With one finger, he pushed up the brim of his green fishing hat. He didn't blink. He just kept looking, like something had clicked inside his head about me. The force of him so strong, it shoved me back.

We picked up our pencils.

His pencil scratched my surface. I drew for my life, the paper too small, like it couldn't contain the entire Trey, like there were pieces inside I couldn't fit. I worked hard and fast like him, focusing on his keen eyes. Every time they flicked up, I wanted to catch them, make them stay forever on me so I could understand him.

I thought again of the spray. I wanted to take out the can, ask him: *Where did you get this?*

I felt other kids starting to watch, taking sides.

Mr. Garci noticed; he came near. "This isn't a competition, you know," I heard him say.

"Yeah, 'cause we know who's gonna win," Trey muttered.

"Yeah, me," I said.

Behind me, jingles of laughter.

Trey slashed hard, dark lines, and ripped out the page. "I'm done with this," he said. I took a sharp breath—my eyes filled every inch; underneath, the circles, looked like smoke.

I put my drawing down. He stared at it.

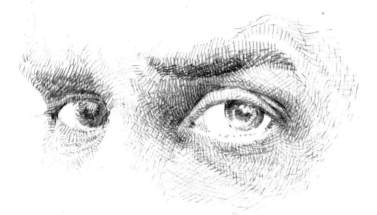

"Very good, Ror," Mr. Garci said.

Trey collected his stuff and left. Garci didn't stop him.

I won. Trey's whole body said I did. I closed my book, dread sinking in me. Damn, after this, he would never talk to me again. That wasn't what I meant to do. When Garci turned away, I slid Trey's drawing between two pages, keeping a shred of him.

15

NOW IT WAS stuck in me—his drawing, his painting, him, like I'd consumed an arrow and felt it leading me. I had to go look at that painting again, even if it meant I might get caught. I had to figure out his letters, copy them into my pad, have them, keep them. Get them right.

There was something about Trey and me that was alike, and I had to figure out what.

I snuck into the building and quietly felt my way upstairs. Outside the room, I heard voices and stopped. They were there, just as I suspected they'd be. I stepped next door and put my ear near a hole in the wall. I wished it was me in that room.

". . . whoever did this, we gotta kill him, we can't let him get away with it," a guy said.

"I bet it was fuckin' Frankie," said a deep voice.

"I don't think so. This don't look like Frankie," said Trey.

I heard, "Yeah, it's Poison Crew, let's get 'em all."

"They pinching our stash again."

"The person did this, they gonna die," Trey said. There was calm in his voice, a kind of killer calm. "Spray *my* piece with *my* best can? That don't fly."

They were talking about what I did. Only they were blaming it on some guy named Frankie. Some poison crew.

Trey spoke again. "Now I have to hit up Jonathan's store and get more," he said. "He's the only one carries that ebony black Krylon."

Jonathan's?

"Man, ain't no free ride at Jon's no more. He's a paranoid freakazoid," a voice said. The deep voice with a crack in it. I tried to see who it belonged to through the hole. I glimpsed that kid with long, curly brown hair.

"Yeah, I was in yesterday, and he went all store detective on me," said a guy I couldn't see.

"I got a feeling it wasn't Frankie, just like you, Trey." A girl's voice. A girl? I almost lost my cover trying to see her. "I got a feeling there's somebody else, some skinny-ass addict or something."

"Nah, they don't spray like that. They too busy gettin' high. I think it was somebody tryin' to prove they better than me," Trey said.

My legs felt watery. I breathed quietly next to the hole, wishing my heart wouldn't beat so loud.

"Ah, shit, let's go bomb that fuckin' Frankie's territory," Deep Voice said. "Let's finish this war." The voice cracked on *war*.

War? They were talking about territory. This was bigger than I thought.

Trey walked back and forth past the hole. Finally, he said, "Yeah, okay, let's go." I heard something being thrown into a bag, their footsteps going away, out the door, down the stairs. The building silent, the sound of traffic in the distance.

I looked at the can of black. What were they going to do? Fight with spray?

I put the can on the ground, and left it there.

16

TREY'S SEAT WAS EMPTY. Mr. Garci started class with a talk about urinals.

"Who can tell me what's so special about a urinal?" he asked.

A wild giggle flared up. Once, we found a Dumpster of urinals, and Dado built a sculpture with them. That's when I started calling him "Dado," after the Dadaists from the 1920s, these artists who made sense with nonsense. *They were so far out, they were in*, Dado said.

"Without urinals, piss goes on the floor," a girl said.

"How would you know? Ever used one?" cracked a boy.

"No, but apparently neither do you boys, the bathroom stinks so bad!"

Arguments broke out, who was more stanky, something about opening legs and taking a whiff—

Garci clapped his hands, shouted, "Fine, fine, this is going nowhere!" until everybody settled down. "Okay, back to the discussion."

"Urinals have kind of a cool shape," someone behind me offered.

"That's a start," Mr. Garci said. "Can we say they're beautiful? Who's to decide?"

I spoke up. "Duchamp."

"Do who?"

"Doo-doo!"

They all burst out laughing.

Garci gave them the look and they shut up. He said, "Duchamp? Did you say Duchamp, Ror?"

I shrugged. I'd said enough.

"It's a miracle, someone's thinking! What about Marcel Duchamp, Ror?"

"Psycho don't know nothin'," a girl behind me muttered.

I said slow and clear: "He put a urinal in a gallery and called it 'Fountain.'"

"Yes, excellent, very good, Ror. Do you remember what he signed it?"

I said, "R. Mutt." Snorts and snickerings. I always signed my comix R. Stegall, like the coolest comix guy in the world, R. Crumb. You think I'd ever tell anyone that?

Trey came in wearing sunglasses. He threw himself into the chair next to me. I glanced over and saw, behind his glasses, that his eye was swollen shut. My heart wobbled. Shit, it was a *real* war, and he'd gotten hurt. I quickly looked away, picked up my pen.

"Ah, so nice of you to join us, Mr. Winthrop," Garci said to Trey, not smiling. He turned back to us. "So, Duchamp exhibited that piece in 1917," he went on. "He signed it, put it on a pedestal in a gallery, and called it art. A radical, shocking act for that time period."

Trey opened his book and held up the side cover so I couldn't see what he was drawing. I wanted to write him a note. *I'm sorry.*

"So, what was the point?" Mr. Garci asked.

"They wanted to break some stupid rules?" a kid said.

"Close, very close!" Garci was excited that someone else had taken a decent stab at an answer. "Duchamp thought everyday objects could become art," he went on. "He named them 'readymades,' and started a whole movement of people turning junk into art by putting it into a gallery space and calling it art. It was the *space* that made it art."

All Dado was missing was a gallery, I thought.

As Garci lectured, Trey finally let go of the cover of his book, deliberately, slowly, so I could see what he had drawn. It was my Fire Pop. Just like the one I'd sprayed on the wall over his painting.

Except he drew it better than me.

I opened my mouth, feeling my whole face flame up. *Damn this guy.*

He took off his sunglasses, watching me. I turned away and pretended I didn't see his black eye.

"You got something to say, Staten Island?" Trey growled low.

Staten Island—I was so tired of that joke. *You came from where? Thought nobody did. The Nobody Island.* Unlike *Manhattan* island, where everybody was somebody.

Well, I lived here now.

I growled back, "Don't call me that."

"What are you gonna do?" he said. I felt Garci starting to look—he didn't like to be interrupted.

"At least I haven't been living in a roach motel all my life," I muttered.

"What do you know about me?" Trey said. When I didn't answer, he said, "You know, you think you all butch like Sigourney Weaver in *Alien*, but you ain't nothin' but a soft yellow banana."

I heard giggles behind me.

Yellow? Banana?

"Trey? Ror? We have a problem?" Mr. Garci asked.

"Nah, it's all right, Mr. G," Trey said. "Me and *Aurora* here, we just talking about some tropical fruit that can't stand the heat." He stuck the sunglasses back on, pulled his leather cap down, and turned a cold shoulder.

I spent the rest of class with my arms folded against myself, trying hard to ignore what I couldn't, what I knew—that I was the cause of Trey's black eye—and he would never let me into his too-cool world. I felt it boiling in me. *Soft. Yellow.* I wasn't scared of him. He wasn't better than me. I didn't care if I started any goddamn war. Why did they have to go to war if he knew it was me, anyhow?

At the bell, I skipped Spanish and shouldered my loads

of homework, weighed down, sick and tired, like I needed a good long vacation on that Virgin Island in that show *Lifestyles of the Rich and Famous.*

I didn't want to go home, where Ma absorbed TV rays on high and fiercely knitted hats she hoped to sell. Instead, I went upstairs to the school library to get some peace.

Too many kids messed around in the stacks, so I gave up drawing and walked down the stairwell. I threw open the door to freedom, and what I saw made me shout, "Oh, shit!" I did a double take and stared at the door, wondering if I was in the right place, feeling the world turned upside down.

Spray-painted in two tones right on the door to Cady High was a Fire Pop—only it was *me*, a perfect portrait of me with dark circles under my eyes. Me running, and from my head, all the way up the door frame, flames and smoke whirling high onto the white brick.

"Oh, damn." It was beautiful—*he made me see myself.*

"Oh, God." It was horrible—*everyone in school would see me.*

I ran all the way to our building, taking the stairs up by twos, past my own floor to the sixth. Outside 621, I stood heaving in and out, dripping sweat. I raised my fist to knock, ready to give him a piece of my mind, when I heard a thud against the door, from the inside. A woman cried out. Another thud. I stumbled back. Behind the door, I heard, "Stop, stop it, James, don't do that!"

A thud, and another thud.

"Stop it, boy!"

Thud, thud.

Something curdled inside me. I backed away, and hurried downstairs.

17

I FELT LIKE I was going nuts. Lunchtime, I steered clear of the food fight in the cafeteria. Up on Broadway, the homeless spread themselves over the benches like sunbathers in Hawaii. A solar-powered day near the end of April, and I wore only my sweatshirt. I flipped the hood over my cap. There was nowhere for me to eat my peanut butter sandwich in peace. I went into the Golden Arches and claimed a booth near the door, hoping they wouldn't send me away. I took out my eats and the sketchpad Jonathan had given me.

What kind of clown would steal an idea?

Ideas were so intangible, so *pffft*. Anyone could pick one up and walk away with it, make it a whole lot better. No fingerprints left behind.

I was really getting into my drawing when I heard, "Yo."

Trey, in his sunglasses. Behind him were the two boys and girl from school, from the abandoned building. The way they were looking at me made my stomach ache. I shouldn't have come here, where they hung out. I closed my book.

"Ain't it sweet of you to save us a place. Now, why don't you move over," Trey said. The boys smushed me into the wall. Trey slid into the booth across from me. The girl sat next to him.

I knew their names from classes. The long-haired, deep-voiced guy in English, Reuben, his eyes dark and round, lived with his grandma in the projects. Nessa, she talked too loud in Spanish, tossed her hair like a *Cosmo* girl, wore gold hoop earrings. Popular with the bossy girls. Kevin, some kind of white-Asian mutt, long like a string bean, always on a skateboard—he sat drawing at the back of world history and flirted with girls who would never go out with him. I bet they knew all about the painting on the school door. I bet they helped Trey do it.

"Tell me, Staten Island, you ride here on a horse?" Trey said, putting a fry on my book. The others smirked. He took a bite of his burger and chewed.

I flicked off the fry and it hit his shoulder. "Hey, I told you, don't call me that."

"Oh, snap!" Reuben said.

"Dis!" said Nessa.

Trey smiled, then threw another fry at me.

"Trey!" she said. "Stop feeding the animals."

Some look passed between them. My belly took a flop. They were a couple. I didn't know what I was hoping.

Reuben, did he know how to blink? Nessa glared at me. Trey, in his leather cap, watched me as he unfolded a piece of paper, one of my Fire Pops. He must've picked it up off the street. "Painted on the wall of our hangout," he said. "Look familiar to you?"

I shrugged.

He went on, "I'm starting a new series. Guys with they head on fire. I call them the Jackson-Pryor Triptychs."

"Jackson-Pryor?" I asked.

"Michael Jackson, Richard Pryor. Heard of them? Celebrities on fire," he said. A slight smile glimmered in his eyes. "My triptych's gonna trip you out."

"That would be a diptych," I said. "A triptych is a series of three paintings, not two, genius."

"Well, thank you, Professor. You look like your head was on fire," he said, leaning in to me, the smile gone. "Maybe you be the third painting."

"Ho, snap," Kevin said.

"Maybe I'll take you with me next time I burn shit up," I said to Trey.

He pulled off the sunglasses and stared at me with his bloodshot eye, like another contest, like who would look away first.

His girlfriend threw her Big Mac on the table and stood

up. "*Caramba*, enough of this," she said. "Let's go." The boys stood up with her, but Trey didn't.

"Nessa," Trey started, but she sucked her teeth and took off. Trey pointed to Kevin, who headed out after her. Reuben slid back in, next to me. Trey threw down the sunglasses, staring at me while he chewed. That look, I couldn't take it, accusing and cocky all at the same time. I opened my sketchpad to avoid it. She knew, Nessa, what I was feeling. I'd seen it before, the lime-green ooze of jealousy. It's totally physical, the way a regular old girl turns into a vicious, man-eating girl when her boyfriend's at stake. First, she's Dr. Jekyll. Then she's Mrs. Hyde.

"What's that?" Trey asked.

"Just a drawing," I said.

"Let's see what else you got in that book," he said.

I flipped through and showed him the one of his eyes I did in class. "Don't worry, they're all of you, Trey. Just like you can't stop drawing me."

"You're lucky I didn't kick your ass for going over my piece and stealing my shit, Ror."

I kept my voice low. "I didn't mean anything by it."

He stared into me until I looked down. "Took me all night to do that."

"Yo, I didn't know," I said.

Reuben said, "Let's get outta here, man."

Trey said, "Don't let it happen again."

He pushed his tray across the table at me. On it was his uneaten bag of fries. As I watched him walk away, I stuffed a whole handful into my hungry mouth.

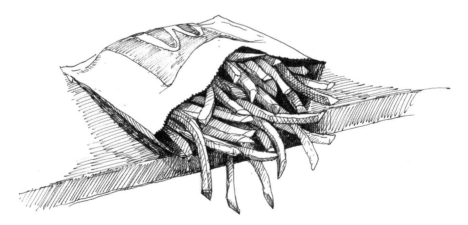

18

I WOULD NEVER be a Norm. I just didn't know how to act. I was a girl raised by fucking hyenas, an uncivilized creature who didn't know how to talk to real people. I saw it now—TV taught you how to get along, showed you what to wear and how to do your hair. It taught you what you *should* look like. With TV, you didn't need to think. You knew which lines to laugh at. I'd missed years of watching. Now it was too late for me. I was just a primitive. A mute. A primate.

At school, I heard them talking about the painting of me on the door. Reuben sat behind me in English class, bragging to someone how he and Trey did it right in the middle of the school day. Kevin passed me in the halls with a girl and pointed me out to her. I looked the other way. Trey lived upstairs; why couldn't I knock on his door? Ask him—

what?—to show me how to spray-paint? But life wasn't a half-hour TV show, and it wasn't so easy to get in with them.

Marilyn had the opposite problem; boys followed her like clouds of mayflies. Since she was a senior at the end of the year and her hand had healed, she got an after-school job at the Carvel on 72nd. She put money away for college, bought our groceries and subway tokens, paid our bills, and at night, she took her new friends out to listen to bands downtown. I didn't want to work at any ice-cream joint. I didn't know what I wanted, but not that. Not slaving for the man in some dumbass job. There had to be another way to make money.

I spent time in the library on Amsterdam Avenue looking for copies of the books I lost in the fire. It was hard to concentrate with this smelly guy picking his bare toes in the art section, this lady breast-feeding her baby on the floor. I checked out an armful on Surrealism and Dada and Pop, and couldn't wait to get home to read about Lichtenstein, the artist who painted comic book characters on ten-foot canvases.

Turning the key to our door, I heard a moaning sound and found Ma at the table, sniffling like she was sick. I put down the books. She was crying. Ma didn't cry, not usually, not ever. What happened with Dado made her disappear inside herself, not cry.

"What's the matter, Ma?"

"Oh, Ror, they're saying it was a suicide."

A flutter of panic rose up in me, like extra heartbeats. "Who said that?" I asked. I slipped into the chair beside her. I handed her a napkin, and she dried off her tears, her staccato breaths slowing in gulps until she stopped.

"Your father's life insurance, from Dow Chemical," she said.

"What, why does it matter?" All this time, we'd never talked about Dado. Never. What life insurance?

Ma sighed, pinching the napkin to the bridge of her nose. "The lawyer said they won't pay out on a suicide." I noticed for the first time gray hairs nestled among her black curls.

I shook my head. "What lawyer?"

"Marilyn thought we should fight it. I thought she was right. We've been fighting to get the insurance money, Ror. A hundred thousand."

What was going on?

Ma smacked the table. "This is why we left the city in the first place," she said. "He was right all along about these companies. They're bloodsucking, controlled by greed, the lot of them."

He was right all along? That's what she thought?

She pressed her palms to her cheeks. "I didn't see it coming, not this, not what we've fallen into. Welfare. Food stamps. I thought we could do it all ourselves."

Her skin had puffed from all the junk she used to fuel herself—*Days of Our Lives*, Pepsi, crullers from Dunkin' Donuts. But she still wore the same lucky earrings: wire hearts Dado had made her from found electrical copper.

"Ma, can I ask you a question?"

Her eyes were red from crying.

I forced out the words: "Why didn't you do something?"

She looked down at her chapped hands and shook her head slowly. "I couldn't help him, Ror. Nobody could. His sickness was like that. I couldn't stop him, and then it got too bad. I never thought he would . . . I never thought it would come to this." She reached out and caressed my arm. "I'm sorry, Rora. I know you miss him most."

My eyes prickled with little needles. I shook off her hand.

"We don't need their money," I said fast. "We'll find a way."
Dado—how could he have left us with nothing? *I'm going to
save you, girl. How? We must fight for what we want and win. We will
build it ourselves. Each step must have a purpose.*

We won't trust anyone. We won't need anyone.

Ma said, "It's all we've got, Ror. That insurance is ours, and I'm going to fight for it."

I felt like I was at the bottom of a well, drowning, clutching for air, something going on so far above me, I couldn't do anything about it.

Suddenly, I let go.

Like I plummeted, like another consciousness dawned on me, separated from me, leaving a shell of me behind. Like Aldous Huxley, like William Blake, like Carlos Castaneda wrote, like the doors to perception were wide open and I was seeing my *doppelgänger*, my body double, only she wasn't there, *it* was.

That portrait of me painted right on the school door. My alter ego.

Follow your purpose.

At fourteen, the Age of Reason, I had declared it at a family meeting.

I wanted him to know: I was an artist.

I wanted to tell my father what I felt deep down—that when I saw what Trey did, I had a vision of how being an artist might work. When I picked up that can of spray and marked the wall, for the first time in my life I felt it was right. I didn't feel trapped by what came before me, or what would come after. I didn't feel contained by the paper, the charcoal, the pen. I felt, for the first time, I had enough space. I was free.

I had to find a way to show that to Trey.

19

AS WE WALKED to the subway, I was thinking how I might hear it on a talk show: *Here's some advice for depressed and possibly psycho-visual, hyper-creative, overly individualistic parents: Don't commit suicide. It's messy, and you leave behind the saddest family on earth.*

Ma and Marilyn led the way. I wasn't looking forward to getting into that sardine can, but we had to sign some papers at the lawyer's office. Since Dow insurance didn't want to pay out—they'd found gasoline on the premises, evidence it was used on the dome, evidence of a suicide—Lawyer Jones was going to try to prove we spent fifteen years building the homestead. We'd file for squatter's rights, adverse possession of the four acres of the King Kennedys land, then Ma could sell it, then we could get some money.

Dado's body was never found. Teeth, bones, turquoise fucking jewelry, all of it gone. Incinerated. Down the steps,

I was thinking: *How are we ever going to bury him?* Through the turnstile, I was thinking: *How can I forgive him?* On the platform, I was thinking: *If I could just see him, I could, possibly, understand.*

And then there he was, right over a bench. I blinked and stopped walking. Marilyn and Ma sat down, not even seeing it. I stared until it became clear that I wasn't just imagining what I saw on the wall of the platform right behind them, big as life. The painting of Dado with his head on fire. And beside him, me—me with my head on fire.

It was a message. In code. From Trey. Only I didn't know what it meant.

Marilyn said, "Ror, you all right?"

I tore my eyes away, and met her confused look. Wind blew into the station, whipping up loose trash, and the train roared in. I took a last look before I followed them on, and stuck close to the door so I could get off quickly if I had to. It creeped me out, this hurtling through space.

The car was decorated everywhere you looked. It calmed me. Felt like Trey was trying to reach me. I traced some of the letters on the door with my finger.

When Marilyn saw what I was doing, she said, "Blech, don't touch that graffiti! Will they ever clean up these walls?"

Graffiti.

Ma shook her head. "That wasn't here when I was a kid. They kept the subways clean."

"It's not *that* bad," I said.

Ma's eyebrows went up. "Not bad? I thought you had more taste, Ror. Look at this mess."

"Yeah, well, look at that one." Behind a row of heads blossomed round purple and blue and black letters that spelled out MIRAGE. "You can't say that's ugly," I went on. "I mean, it's alive like, I don't know, punk rock. It's better than some Budweiser ad."

"It's awful," Ma said. "There's nothing good in it."

Marilyn shook her head like she was starting to put some-

Just for the hate of it.

thing together: The paint can, the graffiti on the school. Had she recognized me? "It's a waste of talent," she said.

I kept my mouth shut. The only one who would understand was Trey.

20

AS SOON AS we got home from the lawyer's, I went back to the abandoned building. I brought my drumbeat brown pen that colored a page antique sepia, and my sketchbook. I went to the top floor, sat across from Trey's painting, and, looking away from the black mark I'd left, started to draw.

I let my hand follow his lines, the strange shapes they made, trying to decipher his code. I found myself diving and swooping along with his curves, falling into the inside of his mind. That's what I loved about art—you could see the inside of someone's mind made manifest. There on the wall, Trey was chaotic and straight, surprising and predictable.

I drew until the sun drained out of the room, until I couldn't see anymore. I drew in the dark, with only the amber streetlight outside illuminating.

Then I heard someone shout, "Police! Put your hands up!"

"Oh, God!" I scrambled to my feet as someone stomped in with a huge flashlight.

Behind it, he started laughing. Trey. He set down a duffel bag. "You scream like a baby girl," he said. I held in my fast breaths and dropped back down on the floor. He shined the light at me, at my book. "I knew I'd find you here," he said.

"And I knew you'd come." I tried to control my crazy heartbeat.

"Yo, Ror, you know what bothers me about you? You act like you the only one in the world with troubles."

"You started this competition, not me."

"Then you ain't got no idea how you look at people," he said. "You with that *glare* all the time."

"You painted my Fire Pop on the platform!"

He came over and kneeled down where I was sitting. With the light, he matched my drawing with his painting on the wall. He took hold of my chin and said, "What you did wasn't right." I thought he was going to punch me; I'd punch him right back. Then I thought he might kiss me deep and hard on the lips, and I was scared I'd latch on to him for dear life and never let him go.

"Don't touch me," I forced myself to say. But I didn't move his hand away.

"You want to be better than me, but you ain't." He shook my head once, then relaxed his grip and let go.

"*Aren't*. You *aren't* any better than me, either," I said.

"Yeah, I can talk whitey. You think you smart, but there's a lot more shit to learn on these streets than on any fuckin' horse farm on Staten Island."

"Trey," I said, taking a breath to let the insult go, "you're wrong. I don't think I'm better or smarter than you," I said. "The truth is, I respect you. Except when you act like a jerk."

He sat back on his heels and stood the flashlight up between us. "The way you draw me," he said softly, "I can't figure out *what* the fuck's goin' on with you."

"You're not so easy yourself," I said.

The hardness in his eyes left then, and I could see inside, fathoms. "That first day you came to class," he said, "you smelled like fire."

"It stays on you," I said. "My dado burned our house down."
It didn't come out easy. "He died. In the fire. That's what the
drawing is. Was. Fire Pop."

Trey was paying attention now.

"My pops left us." He coughed as if something stuck inside him was coming loose.

"Where'd he go?" I asked.

Trey stared into the flashlight. Then, he said, "How the
hell should I know?"

"That how you ended up at the roach hotel, too?"

He met my eyes. "Me and my moms and James, we
wouldn't be in this messed-up situation, hadn't been for
him."

I said, "At least he's alive. Maybe one day you'll find him
and give him hell."

Trey gave me an awful look. He stood up, stretched out his legs, pointed the flashlight at the painting.

"Maybe not," I muttered.

"Your pops teach you to draw?" Trey asked.

"He taught me everything." I stared at the painting on the wall. "Who taught you?"

Trey shrugged. "I got my mentors."

Mentors.

"Hey, listen," I said quickly, "I'm sorry. I've been wanting to say that since I did this. I'm sorry for stealing, I'm sorry for crossing out your painting—I didn't mean to." His back was to me; made it easier to talk to him. "I love it, Trey."

He turned, and I saw his face. How my words affected him.

I saw my chance to ask what I wanted. "Will you take me with you, next time you go?"

He knelt beside me again. "What? You saying you wanna *come*?" he asked. "You one crazy white girl."

"You one crazy black boy."

He laughed.

"Is it scary to paint where anybody can see you?" I asked.

His eyes turned pure. "You don't get no freer than painting where everybody's gonna see it," he said.

"Take me."

"No, there *is* one thing better, Ror. Their faces. Nothin' like seeing the people dig on a fresh painting. Colors in their eyes."

"I want to go."

"You don't know what you asking for," he said, throwing a piece of glass. He had something I wanted so bad, and he knew it. "It's dangerous, specially for a girl. You can't act stupid. Can't let the cops catch you."

"I'm not afraid of the pigs," I said. I thought of how I screamed when he pretended to be police—it was surprise, not fear. Dado trained us to avoid the pigs like hell. All those times scavenging, we never got caught.

Trey tore at a ragged hole in his jeans. "I can't decide alone, anyways."

"What do you mean?"

"You want to be part of the crew, you gotta ask the crew. Noise Inkorporated. We been together three years. I'm the president, but it's a democracy. We take a vote. Reuben's the vice president, Kevin's the treasurer, Nessa's the whole fuckin' senate. We all gotta have a powwow to decide on new members."

Sounded familiar. Trey being president meant he was in charge. "Listen," I said, "I just want to try it one time."

He dug into the floor with some glass. "You don't just come for the ride. This ain't no cruise—it's a crew. Once you're in, you're in."

"Please? I won't tell anybody. I swear I'm not a quitter."

"Shit," he said. He laughed. "You ain't even got no paint."

"I'll owe you, I'll pay you back." I talked fast. "I can't stop thinking about it. I'll do whatever it takes."

He stood, pushed back his cap. "Aight, aight, girl. You

want paint, I'll give you paint." He walked to the duffel and pulled out a paint can. But it was a one-gallon can of white wall paint. He got a roller from the bag and held it and the can out to me. "You want in, you do over this wall you fucked up. Whitewash it, and then I'll think about giving you spray."

I stood up, and I noticed Trey was not much taller than me. I took the roller.

21

BEFORE I BLOTTED out the graffiti with the white noise, I tried to follow how the letters went, the way they linked together, the outline, the shape of it.

"I still don't see what it says."

"It's wild style, child. You don't want every asshole reading your tag."

"I'm not every asshole," I said.

"First letter: R," he told me.

Stepping back, I saw it—like an Escher etching, the R folded like origami, trying hard to fit in.

"Oh, I see it. And this?"

"O."

R-O?

"What's it spell?" I asked.

He ran his fingers over the letters. "ROI 85. My tag."

"That your code name?"

"That's what I write in the street. *Roi* means 'king' in French."

"Like LeRoi Jones? Like Martin Luther King?" I asked.

He whistled. "You up on your black heroes, ain't you? My pops called me Roi. He was a rude boy from the islands."

"A rude boy like Bob Marley?"

In a perfect Jamaican accent, Trey said, "Jah Rastafari, he forget me not."

I said, "I saw Bob Marley play in Central Park once."

"We're jammin'," Trey sang, and danced a reggae move.

"I think I saw you there," I said with a grin.

He laughed.

I said, "So, what's the eighty-five?"

"Our street."

"And this?" I ran my fingers along smaller letters on the outer edge. NOISE INK. "That's the name of your crew!"

"Very good. Now get to work."

I opened the gallon with my knife, dipped in the roller and held it up, letting the thick paint drip back into the can. I didn't want to cover up his painting. He went out of the room and came back carrying a ladder and hung the can off the top. I climbed up and got to work. As I rolled, Trey lit a cigarette and studied the blank whiteness I was creating. As he took colors out of his duffel bag, he named them—cinnamon, alligator, night-sky blue. I watched how he chose the cans, popping the colored tops off, placing them out in preparation. He started messing with the cap of one.

"What're you doing?" I asked.

"Changing this to a fattie." He heated a needle with his lighter and stuck it in the hole, twisting it around to make it bigger. "You can use the top off an oven cleaner, too. Just go in Key Food and flick off the caps with your thumb." He took a handful of caps out of his pocket to show me.

"Can I try?" I asked.

"You got your chance with that can you stole," he said.

"Will you ever forgive me?" I asked.

He gave me a cryptic smile and pointed to the wall.

The cover layer I rolled out dried quickly, and he started shaking his first can. I sat on the floor and watched as he sprayed his outline, all hard and straight lines, even the O. It looked crummy at first—"It's just my foundation, gotta get that solid before I start decoratin'"—until he added layers, filling in the lines with colors, putting in a 3-D shadow around it, and flashes of white, like light reflected, sparkles. The room was dense with aerosol fumes, making me cough. I watched the ever-moving arcs of his arm, the way he tested the can, moved it slantwise, or in and out for different effects. I shoved open a window and listened to the *sssssst sssssssst* of the spray, the *rattle rattle* every time he shook the can. I saw what could happen if I had some.

"It's incredible," I said when he was done.

We stood next to each other and looked at his ROI 85. "It ain't perfect," he said.

It was even better than the last one.

He handed me a can of white that was nearly empty. "This is Krylon; it's the best brand you can get. Go spray something in the other room," he said. "That's your fuck-up space."

I didn't want to leave him, but I walked into the hall, then into the room where I'd put the can of black. It was gone. I shook the white. As I watched Trey paint, a phrase had repeated in my head. With the Krylon, I started the lettering on the dirty white walls:

I held the can for longer sprays, trying out the hand moves, feeling the power of my gun. I did the short, close-up bursts that left drips, the side spray in a narrow line, the dots, the stars, the far and fat swerves. I stepped back. Pretty bad. I continued on:

The white gave me a hint of what it might be like with colors, like a shadow self. Clean white on dirty white didn't show so well. White was the opposite of the black I stole. White, all the colors of the rainbow in one.

Bone white.

Trey came in and whistled and shook his head. "You need a lot of practice, shorty."

I said, "I need a tag."

"Yeah, you do," he said.

"So, am I in?" I asked.

He tapped his Camel against his palm, then lit it with his Bic, watching me with those eyes. "It's gettin' late," he said, not answering my question. "Let's blow this place."

As we walked back to the hotel, I told him again in case he forgot: "I want in. I want to be part of the crew." I wanted it more than anything I'd ever wanted.

At my door, he gave me a hand slap, curving his fingers around mine, teaching me to shake by moving his hand around mine. He gave me no promises.

22

NOW THAT I had cracked the code, I was becoming a moth, attracted to the light of graffiti. I took my sketchpad over to Columbus, to the FOR RENT store with its window guard rolled down. Over it, somebody had sprayed TNT. I drew the building, following the jagged rectangles of every brick with my pencil; I drew the metal lines and how the graffiti fit. On Amsterdam, I stopped in front of the poster of a Virginia Slims model holding a cigarette longer than her fingers. I drew her with her black lungs exposed. I drew a half-crushed garbage can, an old woman wheeling a cat in a stroller while singing a little tune. Up on Broadway, I read the tags: BRAZE 1, SKEL, and that ME ONE I saw all over school. I copied them into my book. If Noise Ink took me in, what would be my name?

I didn't know if I'd ever know. When I walked up to Trey

between classes and reached out for his hand, he shook my fingers awkwardly, glancing around like he couldn't be seen giving me the real shake. In art class, I sat next to him and said, "Hey, did you talk to the crew? It's been, like, a week."

"Chill, Ror. We got considerations, deals to work out."

The rough rejection felt like sandpaper in my stomach. I bit my tongue on a sharp reply. Made patterns in my pad from one corner to the other, just to keep from thinking about it.

On the warm May day of our field trip to the Con-Mod Museum, we gathered outside the school, all twenty-eight of us and Mr. Garci. Somebody's mother was there to help him. Garci gave us a lecture about not touching anything, and we started to walk east, through the stone walls of Central Park.

Spring had come for good, the grass bloomed out; its fresh-cut scent broke the air. I felt Dado, the heartbeat of nature, the way I used to live so close to the earth. I reached down to pick a sprig of garlic mustard, its green taste filling my mouth. I could live on the greens that grew here.

"What are you, a goat?" Trey said when he saw me eat it. It was the first joke he had made to me in a week.

"Baaaa," I bleated.

"You gonna kill yourself, eating that stuff."

"Where do you think food comes from?" I said. I offered him a leaf. "Here, try it."

He held up his hand. "If it ain't wrapped in plastic, I ain't eatin' it," he said. "You don't know what dog took a leak on that!"

I picked a dandelion, sniffing in the musk of its yellow head. I held in the urge to throw my legs around a tree, to pull Trey up with me and show him what I knew.

As we walked, all the kids gathered around Mr. Garci. "What was the first thing the Dadaists did in Zurich during World War I? Who remembers?"

"They declared themselves anti-artists," this girl Sarah said.

Dadaists were anti-artists? That had escaped me.

"Right on, Sarah!" Garci said. "They saw art as commerce, they saw markets as the thing that started the war. War killed their families. Greed killed their brothers and sons. They felt the absurdity of being alive."

"That's some deep shit," someone said.

Across the park, back on the street, car exhaust drowned the good smells. "You wanna see absurd?" Trey said to me. "Check that out." He pointed to a fancy car parked outside a marble building, a doorman in brass buttons letting out a bottle blonde with a poodle. She had more money invested in that dog than I'd ever had in my life. "Imagine it here? Right smack on the wall, ROI 85." He pointed exactly where he'd put it. "Then I'd be king."

The rich lady glared at him as if she'd heard.

Up front, Katy said, "I don't get it, Mr. Garci. Those Dada guys. They're artists, but they say they're *not* artists?"

"That's right," Garci replied. "They turn the label inside out to make it mean something again."

I asked Trey, "You think graffiti is the anti-art?"

He shrugged. "One thing for sure—we all wanna be famous."

A metal and glass building rose in front of us—a fluttering flag said: THE CON-MOD MUSEUM.

"The Dadaists weren't thinking about art in this context," said Mr. Garci, indicating the museum. "They were listening to their souls."

Trey slapped his hand against his chest and said, "Soul. Now you talkin' my language, Mr. G, man. Keepin' it real."

The kids around him laughed. *Real.* Revolving through the glass doors, I felt my body weight change, as if I got lighter. Felt like I could see every corner of this sweeping space from somewhere above, like I was standing on an empty stage, waiting for something to happen. As we got on the escalator, I stepped up to Trey. "I could see your painting in here."

He glanced around, shaking his head. "You want to put paintings where nobody's gonna see?" he asked. "Come on, Ror—everybody, even those homeless dudes on the corner, can dig graf. Here, you might as well put it inna closet."

I thought: *In this museum, my drawings would never burn.*

We followed Mr. Garci into a spacious gallery. "Oh!" I said when I saw what was hanging there. "That's what it really looks like."

"What?" Trey said.

"This! I've seen this painting a million times in books!" I stood in front of Dalí's *Persistence of Memory* that seemed to breathe on the wall. Ants eating a pocket watch. Three floppy clocks. A blob face on the ground, a tongue coming from its nose.

Trey gave a low whistle. "This guy's trippin'," he said.

Mr. Garci walked over and said, "This is by a Dadaist who was kicked out of the school because he wasn't Dada *enough*. Salvador Dalí invented his own style and called it 'psycho technique.' You get it? Just by looking at the painting, you can see what he means."

"Was he crazy?" Katy asked.

Sometimes, I just hated that word.

"Funny you should say that. He set himself up for deliberate hallucinations, or visions," Garci said. "I don't think he was crazy."

"Sounds like he was smoking angel dust," somebody joked.

Sounded more like he ate peyote, which they said could make you think you were an angel.

I said to Trey, "I read this theory about angels once. Said they kiss your eyelids when you die, making you forget your whole life before you move into the next body. That's why we don't remember who we were before we came here. Wonder if my dado got kissed. Maybe he's forgotten me already."

Trey gave me one of those dark looks and said, "Angels watch over you. They don't forget."

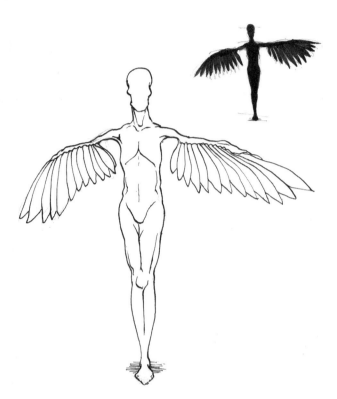

Mr. Garci walked us to another room where we stood before a Frida Kahlo. "I love her. I never thought I'd get to see one of these," I said.

"Check the seagull brow," Trey said.

Frida stared straight into me from the self-portrait doubled in a mirror. Trey got quiet as we looked. Like she reached out and touched us and said *Paint*.

I asked Mr. Garci: "If these Dada guys were so anti-art, how come they're hanging here?"

He kind of lit up. "It's a perfect irony, isn't it, when you think you're the revolutionary, and you end up here. But it's revolution one day, mainstream the next. The Dadaists who lived in 1920 would get sick at the idea of being in this museum almost sixty-five years later. Now look at them. That's history."

As we walked into the next room, Trey said to me, "That's why this place ain't for us. Not while we alive, at least."

"How do people get into a museum, anyway?" I wondered.

"You gotta be rich, white, friends with the right people," he said. "Or you gotta be dead. We ain't dead yet."

"I've got one out of four," I said.

"Yeah, but you're a girl. You may's well be black like me."

"Frida Kahlo's a girl."

"Married to a famous dude."

I stopped short. "So that's what I've got to do to get in a museum? Marry a famous dude? I can't do it on my own?"

"You dream 'bout bein' in the museum till you dead, Ror. I'll take bein' the revolutionary. Let history worry about me," Trey said.

I didn't like that answer. Not one bit.

ANOTHER WEEK WENT BY, and Trey *still* wouldn't talk to me about being in the crew. I'd lose my damn mind, I realized, if I kept thinking about it. Why was it taking so long? Had they decided against me? Why couldn't they just tell me that? Worse yet, when I got to school after the rainy weekend, I saw that the portrait of me on the door was gone, painted over. Just a black hole where I'd been, even the bricks back to white again. Reuben sat on the steps beneath. He drew in a hardcover book with markers.

"Hey, Reuben, where'd it go?" I tried to see into his book.

He tilted the cover closed, holding his place with his fingers. "What?"

"The painting of me."

His eyelids lowered. "What painting?" he said. He looked

around, like I was dumb for talking about it here, in public, with teachers nearby.

"Did Trey black it out?" I asked.

"Yo, I don't know what you're talkin' 'bout!"

Kevin came over and sat beside Reuben and folded his arms and stared at me. Why was everything such a fucking mystery with these guys?

I left them sitting on the steps and went inside. I had to find someone to talk to. Someone outside of the crew I could show my drawings to, someone I could tell about all the letters and pictures and colors I was seeing on the streets. Treasures of art in the ruin of a city.

After school, I headed over to Jonathan's store. He was in the studio, making a frame. When he heard the bell and saw it was me, he wiped his hands clean of glue and came over.

"Long time, kiddo. I was beginning to wonder if I pegged you wrong," he said.

"I was busy."

I put the pad on the counter, and he turned the pages slowly, not saying anything. My eye kept going to the cans there behind him, beckoning like fingers.

If I could buy my own paint, I wouldn't have to be in any freaking crew.

Forget it, I didn't want to be in it anyway.

Jonathan turned the pages harder, like something was

getting him mad. Claws of frustration scraped at me. He closed the book, and I met his watery blue eyes.

"Let me ask you something," he said.

"What's that?"

"You want to be a real artist?"

Felt like he shoved me. I bristled. "What do you mean?"

"I see this—this *crapola*—messing up a good pad I gave you. You want to be a real artist, you don't do this. Not this worthless trash from the street!" He acted as if we'd talked about this a bunch of times before. Who did he think he was, the art police?

My breath tore at my throat in protest. "I think it's beautiful!"

"It's not gonna get you anywhere! Kids writing their names over and over. What kind of talent you need for that?"

Nobody talked to me like that, not anymore. What did he know about it, anyway? He was just some old guy. "It's the space, the color—"

"Look here, you want color, use these." He walked over to a shelf and slapped a set of watercolors onto the counter—a Winsor & Newton set, not baby stuff—and another pad of thick, expensive paper. I stood there, his words working inside me. I felt around my empty pockets, wishing I hadn't spent my last cents on a slice of pizza, wishing I could come up with a way to make money, like with my comix. I didn't want to owe this guy anything. I didn't want him to tell me what to do.

"You got real talent, kid. Don't waste it. Go on, get outta here. Go be brilliant," Jonathan said.

Talent, a waste of talent. Slowly, I reached for the paints.

As I left, I saw it—ROI 85 on the outside wall of the store in a big, angry scribble. Trey's tag. Different from his pieces, those masterpieces I now recognized on the streets. I thought I knew the distinction: With a tag, you made a

claim. With a piece, you showed how great you were. Was it like that?

When I got home, I got a bowl of water, threw myself on the floor with the pad, and accidentally kicked over Ma's pile of secondhand books, which knocked down the tippy lamp she'd found in the garbage, which spilled a half-cup of grape juice in a darkening blotch on the depression-yellow carpet before I could catch it. I felt trapped by the shitty apartment, the flimsy paint, the size of the paper. But the hell with it, I dipped the brush into the bowl, swirled it into the hard square of red until it got creamy, and got started.

I painted the sculptures he built from what we found. Once he nailed together hundreds of discarded thread spools to encase the face of a grandfather clock, then made it tick. Another time, he made a crowd of figures out of crooked driftwood. An audience? There was the plastic packaging melted together into a greenhouse; we used it for seedlings in the spring. The tower of urinals. He didn't limit himself.

The dances I did with Dado those nights he chanted Blake by the Kill, drum strapped around his neck, fire from the pits flickering up his torso while his body bowed and swirled like a fish, a bird. The leaves on the trees in prism pigments I could taste as strong as nutmeg. Kean and Djefa, their sweat on me, our clothes hanging from bushes.

They were scattered all around, my life in pictures.

I thought, *I don't want to end up like him.*

For Dado, *it* never came. *Being famous*—what Trey said.

I pushed aside the watercolors and went up to 621. I stood there, wishing I had the nerve to knock. I put my ear to Trey's door. Inside, I heard the TV. I heard all the TVs on the floor, Ronald Reagan radiating into apartments with his death beams.

In spite of my fear, I reached out and found myself knocking. His mother answered, a spatula upheld, the smell of fried meat coming from behind her.

"Um, is Trey home?" I asked.

She looked into the apartment. "Trey? You home, baby?"

He came to the door. He seemed different: no hat, in a tight T-shirt and shorts. "Yo, Ror, what's happenin'?" he said, reaching out.

I put up my hand for the slap. He gave it to me, curling his fingers around mine. He held on for one extra second, then he let go.

"I just—I came to talk to you," I said.

"'Bout what?" He yawned and stretched out his long muscles.

"About me being in the crew. What's the story?"

He leaned against the doorjamb and folded his arms. "What do you look like without that hat, Ror?" he said softly.

I touched my head, my neck flaming. My hair had grown a whole inch. Still, it was like a blind beautician had gotten to me. "Why?"

He shrugged. "I just wanna know what's under there."

"My brains," I said.

He smiled. "Meet us at the building at midnight," he said. I heard his little brother laugh somewhere behind him, and Reagan's voice repeating on the nightly news: ". . . the homeless who are homeless, you might say, by choice."

"Midnight?"

"Tonight," he said. He stepped back from the door and closed it in my surprised face.

24

MA HAD THE SAME trouble sleeping as me. We stayed up watching TV to wonder at the latest from our senile president who reminded me more of a roach than a person. I drew, and she knitted hats to sell on the street from the contraption that she'd made from an old suitcase and some wheels. My sister snored like a dog on the bottom bunk.

Near midnight, I got up and started to head out. Ma said, "Where are you going, Ror?"

I stopped, my hand on the door. I couldn't remember the last time she questioned me when I went wandering. I thought of telling her I was joining a graffiti crew in an abandoned building in the middle of murderous New York City, but I just said: "I have to go out."

She paused knitting. "For?"

"I can't sleep. I'm going for a walk."

"Give me some direction. Which way are you headed?" she asked. Since when did she care?

"I'm just going to loop down to the river."

She studied my face and said, "There's one thing I have to know, Ror," and my stomach did a double somersault.

"Yeah?"

"Marilyn said someone spray-painted a drawing like yours on the side door of the school. She thinks you did it. Did you?"

I looked over at my Sleeping Beauty sister, restraining myself from putting a pillow over her face. Who knew she had been watching me so closely? "Nope, wasn't me," I said simply. "Anyway, it's gone. They painted it out."

Ma swung back to the TV, where the talking heads bandied words:

Do ya think it's true, Ralph, what Reagan says?

Which part is that, Phil?

What the president is trying so hard to backpedal on: "You can't help those who will simply not be helped . . . the homeless are homeless by choice . . ." Well, are they, Ralph?

I held my breath, waiting for Ma to say more. Was I going to stand here and watch the stuffed shirts all night, or split? When she didn't speak, I turned to go. Then she said: "Ror."

My hand gripped the doorknob. I was going, no matter what.

"Are you getting into that graffiti stuff?"

I hesitated. Then, I said, "No."

"Stay away from Central Park. You're not back in an hour, I'll call Missing Persons."

"Yeah, sure, Ma."

"I'll be waiting."

I left, knowing she'd be asleep by the time I got back. I made my way to the building, and crept over the garbage, in through the basement door. Inside was dark, dead quiet; fear trickled into me. It occurred to me I could get raped or something. Trey had given me no choice but to come to this place. Did I want to spray-paint so badly that I'd go to a deserted building in the middle of the night where I might get attacked?

I took a deep breath, scaled the stairs, and pushed the door open. It was empty, orange from the streetlight. I went inside to wait. Something brushed by me—my arms fluttered up, pushing it away. Suddenly, I was surrounded by the sound of breathing, by warm flesh. I felt them but I couldn't see their faces. I wanted to scream, but it was all stuck inside me.

I smelled coconut and leather.

"Trey? Shit, is that you, man?"

He turned on his flashlight and shined it in my face. I could hear all his buddies laughing at me.

"Psych!"

I said, with my heart still hammering, "What the hell you doing?"

"Just making sure you ain't a perp," Trey said, his voice hard. A what? He put the flashlight on the floor, beam up; now I could see them.

"Dang, looks like the girl nearly peed her Pampers," Nessa said.

They all thought that was hilarious. I just wanted to go paint.

"You stole from us." Trey.

"We don't like that." Kevin.

"We don't trust people who steal from us." Reuben.

"I didn't know it was you!" I said, too loud.

"Step one of this test," Reuben, with that deep voice, intoned.

"What test?" I said.

"You gotta pass our baptism by fire," said Trey. "You gotta rack up some ebony black Krylon from Jon's shop, or we don't take you."

"Rack up?"

"Steal it."

From Jonathan? I choked on the pit in my throat. No way I could get near those cans.

"Nessa goes with you as a decoy," Trey went on. "She'll show you where Jon's is."

I looked over at Nessa, those gleaming bottle-brown eyes. I wasn't going to put my life in her hands. "She hates me," I said.

She snapped, "Who says I hate you?"

"You think I'm trying to take your boyfriend."

She sucked her teeth. "Trey wouldn't touch—"

I cut her off. "I don't want him."

I turned to Trey, and saw in his face that wasn't the right thing to say. *I didn't mean it like that.* Ever since the fire, I felt dead inside, too numb to open myself to boys again. I was too ugly, too screwed up.

I could still feel Trey's hand in mine.

I heard her say, "Yeah, right."

"Why do I have to steal it?" I asked Trey.

Reuben said, "We gotta know you can handle perpetrators and toys."

"Cops and loud-mouth citizens," said Kevin.

"Other crews and lone wolfs who'll try to tear your ass down," Nessa added.

His brow dark, Trey took it up: "The streets is dangerous, the crew does some dangerous shit. We got classified levels, and we gotta know we can trust you with our top secret four-one-one."

Kevin: "You steal it, we got something on you."

And Reuben: "We know you can take on some shit."

I thought about it. Could I be trusted? With what?

"You go tomorrow," Kevin said. "We all cut school and you go with Nessa into Jon's. We wait here."

I protested: "Why do I have to go with *her*?"

Kevin threw down his skateboard like he was going to speed away. "Yo, I'm Audi, man. She's questioning everything we say." He rolled the board.

"This just ain't gonna work out." Nessa fisted up her fingers.

I saw my whole opportunity flushing down the toilet. I held up my hands. "Hey, wait. Hey, I'll do it. I'll go with her. I'll steal the entire store with her, if you want."

Trey said, "Just chill, Nessa. She'll do it, Kev. Give her a chance." He looked at me. "Right?"

They waited for me to answer. I tried to find my cool as I looked around. "Right," I agreed.

25

IT WASN'T THE PIGS freaked me out, it was Nessa. I didn't trust her. In the morning, I decided I wouldn't shoplift with that girl, the hell with it. I'd just tell them forget it. Just do my own thing. I could figure it out somehow.

I put my schoolbooks and my drawing pads in my backpack. When I came downstairs, Nessa was standing outside, bobbing her head to some music. I thought of Trey; he'd know if I bagged out. She was moving to the disco or whatever, and when she saw me, we started walking. I kept waiting for the right moment to tell her that I wasn't going to do it. I could hear the music leaking out of her headphones, surprised by the electric guitar.

I tapped her and pointed to my ears.

She reached in her bag and came out with a cassette case. A mix tape—she'd drawn the cover in a swirly hand. The last song was "I Wanna Be Sedated."

"The Ramones?"

She nodded.

"Man, I'd kill to hear the Ramones." I listened to WPLJ, the home of rock 'n' roll, on the cheap radio Ma got me. I was starved for all the good music I could get.

Nessa took off the headphones and handed them over. As I put them on, I caught a whiff of her bubble-gum perfume. Joey Ramone's voice injected pure energy into me and kept my steps going down the street. Before I knew it, we were half a block from Jonathan's.

Nessa clicked off the music and took the Walkman back. She said, "He's out—his daughter works on Tuesdays. I'll go in first, talk her over to the window. You come in, take the can, split. I'll meet you back here." She looked at me, hard. "Don't screw it up."

I nodded, my belly squeezed tight like a blown-up bag. Too late to say no. As I trailed in after her, I felt super hyper aware of every single detail: the woody gust of pencils and lumber, the murmurs of men by the back, oil tubes in careful cases along the inner wall.

I walked the aisles, listening to Nessa talking, trying to see over the shelves what Jonathan's daughter looked like. Long black hair, a black skirt, fishnets and boots. What if he wasn't really out, what if he suddenly appeared from the studio where he made his frames? Two suits stood by the counter, talking over some foam core, not moving away. I couldn't possibly do it with them there. I could do illegal things, but not with an audience. I preferred gleaning what no one wanted, secret subversions, off-the-grid operations.

Then I thought of Trey. Pretending I was him, I walked over to the counter, went behind it as if I belonged there, and took the can. I smiled at the suits and walked down an aisle and stuck the can in my jacket. I nodded to Nessa and left.

I ran down the block and waited. The cold metal ate straight into my ribs like a disease. Cool as a lily pad, Nessa strolled toward me. When she reached me, she lifted her hand. I slapped her five. I held my breath so I wouldn't puke.

"Wasn't so fucking hard, was it?" she said.

It was. It really was. "Nah," I said.

"It gets easier, sister."

I met her eyes for the first time. Some storms brewing in there. This was one sister who had it in for me.

26

PUNK MUSIC SCREECHED from a huge silver boom box covered with black-inked graf and stickers of bands and foreign flags. Kevin did squats, drop-kick moves with Reuben like a Russian dance, crunching over broken glass. Trey stood by the window in a top hat, blowing out smoke rings and drawing with his fat red Uni in his black book. When he saw me and Nessa watching from the doorway, he walked over. The boys kept dancing.

"You made it," Trey said to us, like he thought we might not.

I took out the can and showed him.

"How was she?" he asked Nessa. She gave him a look like *Why are you asking about her?*

"It was easy," I said.

"Give it up." Trey held out his hand. I gave him the can. He took it and zipped it into his duffel. When he saw my look, he said, "We do it this way 'cause we have to, ain't no other way."

"Yeah, I get it," I assured him. "So? I passed the test? I'm in?"

He blew smoke, measuring my worth with his eyes. He turned away and watched the boys dance, keeping together like they were practicing for something. They were like that Baryshnikov guy with those high side kicks.

"You gotta decide on a tag, sister," Nessa said. She used *sister* like a bludgeon. She pulled a cigarette from the pack in Trey's jacket pocket; he let her. "You gotta decide how you want people to see you."

"What's that mean?"

"It's different for girls, being a graf writer," she said. "It's either—'I'm a girl and I'm a writer,' or 'I'm a writer even though I'm a girl.' Think about that when you pick your tag."

A writer? I never thought of it that way. "What's yours?"

"You seen me on the street," she said, her eyes extra big with attitude. "I'm just sayin'—if you tag some bullshit, that's all you'll be. Not a writer, just a toy who everyone thinks got help from the boys in her crew. Even if *she* was in a crew *before* this fucking crew even *started*." She directed her words at Trey, the bitterness like lemon juice puckering her mouth.

Trey blew smoke hard and stalked away. He turned off the music. The boys stopped dancing. Trey smashed out his cigarette. "Aight, bros. Let's take Ror over to Riverside."

From the way he changed the subject, I saw he didn't know what to do with Nessa's beef, that they'd argued it before, and it had come to nothing.

"Can she climb a fifteen-foot chain-link fence?" Kevin asked, breathing heavy.

"Can she run faster than a dog or a cop?" Reuben pulled his shirt up over his face to wipe off the sweat.

Able to leap tall buildings in a single bound.

Trey looked at me.

"I can do anything you can do," I said to them.

"We'll see," Nessa said.

27

IT WAS TURNING out to be one of those days in late May when all the gnats go for your eyes, a day you don't want to be in school anyway. It was a day you'd rather spend with people who make it seem like flesh is porous and they could be you and you could be them, walking up Amsterdam Avenue past mango-smelling bodegas in the heat rays of the sunshine.

Tags I'd missed came jumping out at me from lampposts, garbage cans, diamond-metal basement covers—like by sudden magic, I could see an X-ray of the world, and these tags were the bones. NOISE INK in block letters, in bubbles, in stars, in sharp angles. Written in a doorway, on the side of a bus shelter, on the mailbox. Up there, where a low roof met a high, I saw in letters big as the Hollywood sign: ROI 85.

Wild excitement volcanoed in me—I knew these guys!—I was walking down the street with them, I was going to be in a crew with them, we would go out together and write our names, and everybody would know who we were. On the street, people were shopping, or keys out, going into their apartments, or walking fast to get somewhere, and I wanted to tell them: *Lift your heads up and look around. Look at us.*

Reuben smacked green-alien stickers onto all the STOP signs. I asked him for one and saw he had drawn the alien right on those peel-off post office labels you got when you sent out a package. I met his eyes and smiled. He nodded, a grin playing on his face. It was like finding my tribe, being with them.

"Aight, Ror, check it out." Kevin braked his skateboard in front of a boarded-up storefront. Sprayed out in sharp, clean white fades with red and gold and green flourishes, it said this:

"What's NIL?"

"That's me, man!"

"Oh! What's it mean—'there's no meaning'?" I said. "How can I not look if I'm already looking?"

He threw his arm out. "She's questionin' me again!"

"Kevin's a nihilist," Reuben explained. "An existential nihilist. Doesn't think this life has any value. Like we're just dust in the universe, man."

"Means he's eaten too many magic fuckin' mushrooms," Trey said.

"That's not it!" Kevin pushed at the air like he was wiping us away. "I just don't think we make any difference."

"We who?" I asked.

"There's all this hype that humans are the superior species and nothing else matters. Especially Americans, like their shit don't stink, like it's all right to fuck up this planet with our nuclear bombs. I think that's bullshit—we're nil, we're nothing compared to what's out there." Kevin pointed up at the sky.

I got the thing about the nuclear bombs, but—"Americans? Where you from, anyway?"

"He's a fucking vegetarian!" Nessa shouted. She took off her headphones, and I could hear Blondie blasting out.

"Kev, shit, we forgot the boom box, man," Trey cried. "Go back and get it!" He grabbed Nessa's headphones and put them on. He started singing and dancing right there in the street, robotic Michael Jackson moves to "Call Me."

Kevin ignored him. "My mom's Chinese and my dad's Italian," he said. "And I'm not a vegetarian."

"They have some good rice at his house," Reuben joked. "Risotto à la tofu, mmm, mmmm, good."

"Get the box, I said, man! What you still doin' here?" Trey yelled.

Kevin sucked his teeth and dropped his board. "I'll catch up to you." He took off.

The neighborhoods changed fast: from Bummy on Broadway to Wealthy on West End. We walked down to the olive-green Hudson River, where the wind churned whitecaps, then back up the drive along the car-stink highway to a park with a chain-link fence towering around it. The gate was locked.

Inside, the concrete walls and handball courts were covered with graffiti. I hung my fingers on the cold links. All different styles, colors, sizes of letters and pictures filled my eyes. I stood there hunting out NOISE INK, or NIL, or ROI 85. It flashed out before me, who these guys behind me were. How much time they'd been together, what they had done while I was back at the King Kennedys digging in the dirt. They'd had a whole lifetime together, and I was trying to join like it was nothing. I felt like a fool, pushing so hard to make me one of them.

Trey said, "Ror, you climb the fence first. Let's see if you can get over."

I looked at them, the little smiles playing on their faces, like they thought I couldn't do it. Could Nessa, in her brighty whitey Adidas? I looked up. The fence was like a million feet high. I hated climbing chain link. "I can do this," I said.

"Let's see." Trey waved his hand.

I tightened my backpack and hooked my boot in a link. The worst part of fences like this was the pointy ends, but at least there was no barbed wire. Still, I'd gotten stuck at the top before. I felt them watching me struggle and grunt, waiting for me to fail. I flipped over, trying not to catch my jeans on the sharp tips, and scaled down inside.

Kevin had caught up with us, carrying the boom box. I stood breathing heavily, waiting for them to come on.

"Good," Trey said. They started walking away.

"What the fuck, where you going?" I cried out, following them from inside.

Kevin turned on the music, and that punk band came on, something like "Ain't got talent, ain't got class, use that hand to wipe your ass—" They all cracked up, slapping each other like crazy. They started singing loud, each shouting a line. All of a sudden, Kevin broke into one of his moves, and Trey spun and jumped as he walked.

"Wait up!" I called.

Nessa and Reuben did some twists together, dancing away, laughing with each other. Ignoring me.

"Where the hell you going, man?" I shouted over the music.

Down a block, the gate was open. They rocked into the park toward me, mouths open in laughter.

I was ready to give Trey a piece of my mind when he said, "You passed your second test."

28

TREY SET DOWN the duffel bag on a bench and zipped it open, the colors a chopped-up rainbow. "Oh my God, is that beautiful," I breathed. Like a symphony, I heard brown Gregorian chants, red cymbals, black timpani. I tasted purple haze, yellow sun sweat. I felt frosty blue, smelled Irish Spring green.

Had they stolen all those cans from Jonathan?

Kevin dug through the bag, muttering, "I need engine red, and some Mean Joe Green."

Reuben grabbed my ebony black.

Trey took mellow yellow, angel white, chocolate brown. He tossed Nessa cans of turquoise blue and girly pink.

When I moved to reach into the bag, Trey held up his hand. "Uh-uh. Today, you be the lookout," he said. "No painting for you." Words caught in my throat. After all I went through, and he wanted me to just sit still? "We need recon, someone to keep an eye out for cops and crooks," he went on. "That be you."

What did he want me to do, walk the perimeter like a paranoid freakazoid or something? I needed to lay my fingers on a cold can and let the spray loose.

Reuben messed with the cap on the black, and got up to a wall. Real smooth, he sprayed out ME ONE in letters that dripped long and curly as his hair. So he was the ME ONE I saw on the street and all over school!

With his free hand, Kevin took out a folded piece of paper and opened it up to a sketch that said NOISE.

"I'm going over Frankie's piece with this," he told Trey. He held it up to the handball court, where I saw POISON painted across the whole wall in these fierce accordion letters. I wanted to go up close and study how they did it.

"Let's kill that shit," Trey said.

Why wouldn't he let *me* have a can?

I slammed myself down on the bench next to the bag and took my drawing pad from my backpack. With a thick gray Design marker I snagged from Garci's class, I started trying out ideas for my new identity.

Nessa came over and said, "Grab a can and get up."

"What?"

She shook her head at me. "Trey said you got mad skills,

but he didn't tell me you were so fuckin' stupid."

Trey said I got mad skills? I squinted at her. "What are you talking about?"

"He's messing with you, sister."

She tilted her two cans slowly like she was holding grenades she was thinking of throwing. The ball bearings rolled back and forth inside.

"I still don't get it," I said.

She clucked her tongue. "You are one dumb bitch. He's playin' with your head. Does it look like any cops around here? This is our teenage wasteland. The boys and me, we do recon all the time—we're always checkin' out the scene, you know, like we got a sixth sense, especially for Frankie." She took a quick look around, like he might be there.

"What do they have against that guy?" Over the wall, Kevin and Trey were already covering Poison's piece with a giant N.

"Fuckin' Frankie thinks he's king 'cause he goes to Art and Design, but he's really just Jabba the Hutt. He ain't like Iz or Lee. He ain't no Dondi."

I had no idea who she was talking about.

She kept on going. "Frankie ain't no kind of famous. That's why I came to Noise Ink. I was in Frankie's crew before, when I lived up on 125th with my moms."

"What's Art and Design?" I asked.

"High school you try out for." With a finger, she circled a name I'd drawn. "Aura's not too stupid. Get a can, let's go."

I picked out Icy Grape, the name on the can. We went to a low wall that held up a hunk of concrete. Nessa sprayed out:

She was TNT? From Columbus Avenue? I studied the letters—it *was* her.

I took a quick look around the park, hugging the can. I'd never sprayed in public. I couldn't bring myself to pop the purple top.

"You waiting for a formal invitation to come in the fuckin' mail?" Nessa snapped.

Dado's warnings rang in my head.

She knelt to the wall and wrote:

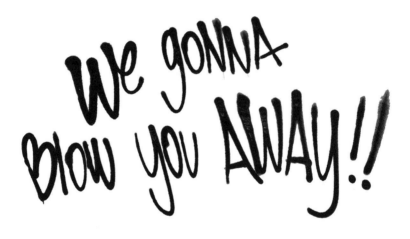

Beside it, fast and clean, she painted a winking girl with big hair.

I took a deep breath, shook the can, and took off the top. I got down to the empty space beside her. I felt them all around me, the crew, working together on their separate parts of the big whole. Together, the crew, like a commune.

The first shot of spray jolted me. I chased the paint up and around, trying to stay with it, the speed of it blasting the wall, splatters landing in my open mouth like bitter grape juice. Purple had a sound all its own, like a magic trick, *ta-da!*

I tried to push off the feeling we weren't alone, that there was someone watching.

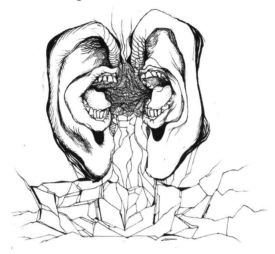

But who? An invisible pressure from behind, pigs in the shadows, spooks in the trees—made me stop and turn around. The crew busy over there, making paintings.

"Where's your tag? What's with the ears? This ain't no fuckin' chalkboard," Nessa said.

I sprayed out real quick:

The word was like marking Z for Zorro, like finding the guts to dive into a cold pool, like *Fuck, I did it!*

Everyone took a break; they'd come over and were watching me—I could hear the music from the boom box. I stepped back to look, glancing at them. I couldn't tell by their faces if I was any good at this.

I said, "So?"

Nobody answered.

Then, Kevin: "You got style, but look at these broken lines here. You got lazy hands, Ror." He pointed out a section of the name where I lost control of the can and hoped no one would notice.

"This here," Reuben said. "You should be filling this in." He showed me an area I could have used to better effect.

"I still don't know about that freaky picture." Nessa put her hands on her hips.

I waited for Trey to say something. He took off his top hat, put it on the ground, and sprayed the crown yellow. He put it back on his head and walked away. I picked another spot on the wall and started again.

29

THE PROBLEM WITH GRAF painting is that it stinks. The smell of spray gets in your skin, your clothes, your hair. If you love spray, you love that reminder. But it was half-witted to show up at dinnertime, Ma and Marilyn at the table already twirling their pasta, watching news on the TV.

I served myself a plate and sat down, suddenly way too aware of how I smelled.

Marilyn lifted some spaghetti up to her mouth. She said, "Ror wasn't in school today."

I glared at my sister. Ma kept watching TV—*Princess Diana attends a charity gala, with Luciano Pavarotti singing*—I wasn't sure she heard.

"You better watch out, snitches get stitches," I muttered to Marilyn.

My sister stuffed her mouth and chewed. She broke up a

meatball while examining me: the colors between my fingers, the splatters on my jean jacket. Who could eat with those eyes on them?

"What?" I said.

Marilyn took a sniff. "I'm just wondering why you weren't in school, Ror. I mean, after all the tests you took to get in, and—"

"What do you care?" I swirled the spaghetti in the red sauce. How many times had I skipped classes and no one seemed to notice? Shit, I hadn't even gone to school until now, and it hadn't seemed to matter much.

"Ror?" Ma woke up. "You weren't in school?"

"School's important, little sister," Marilyn said.

"Bullshit."

"Ror, what's going on?" Ma's voice made my stomach hurt. She got up and turned off the TV. She didn't sit back down. For a second, I saw the old Ma who used to ask me questions all the time.

I took a breath and pushed around a meatball. "I—some—some painters in my school were doing a project, and I wanted to be a part of it." That sounded good, right?

"Painters? What kind of painters?" Ma asked.

Marilyn slurped up some long strands, her eyes wide open, waiting for the answer.

"Ma? You know how Dado—" His name, it made Ma choke, like ripping off a heart scab. What was I going to say? "Dado wanted me to learn about art in a classic sense. I mean,

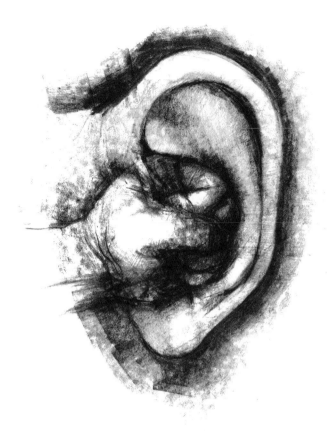

he taught me about Brancusi and Calder. The purity and the balance. But his own sculptures—I just don't know what he wanted to *do* with them."

Marilyn side-eyed me. She knew I was deliberately avoiding the question.

But Ma answered. "Peter always felt torn between utility and beauty." She stopped and shook her head. "Why are you bringing up your father now?" That look in her eye scared me like a switchblade.

"Well, Dado had four acres to work with, he had tools and wood and things he could scavenge. But I don't make things like him. All I have are these little rectangles. I—I always felt that paper wasn't big enough."

Ma folded her arms around her waist as if to hold herself in. "What's all this got to do with school?"

I shook my head. "Now I know—that's—that's why Dado brought me a whole roll that night."

"What night?" We never talked about that night. Even with all the stuff going on with the insurance and the lawyers and the property, we never talked about anything. TV did all our talking for us.

"That night. That night. He brought me that big roll of paper," I said, "and he kicked it so it rolled all the way across my room. Like it was a *path*, a path to *somewhere*. He said, 'I'm going to save you, girl.' Then he left, and that was the last time I saw him." I forced the words out, trying to control the bee stings inside me. "I could never figure out what he meant."

They both stared at me. In a shaky voice, Ma said, "He did that?"

"Right before he went downstairs and started the fire." My fingertips were icy grape. I rubbed my mouth and said, "Now I know what he meant."

"God, what could he have been thinking?" Ma said to herself. I heard in her voice all the sadness for not getting to him, not fixing him. *Why didn't you help him, Ma?*

"I think he was showing me a path to here." It sounded simpleminded, but that's what I felt.

She shook her head, not understanding.

"Ma, I joined a crew of painters. We paint on the street," I said.

She blinked quickly. "A crew?"

"Graffiti, I knew it!" Marilyn said. "They run around in those crews."

Ma's face went dark, her eyes hardened. "Ror, I asked you about that, you said you weren't doing it."

"I wasn't. Before this."

"I don't want you getting mixed up in all that."

"Ma, you're the one taught me about being a revolutionary!" I shoved back my plate. It banged into my glass. "Why are you giving me a hard time about this?"

"A revolutionary?" Marilyn said.

"A revolutionary!" Ma said wonderingly. "Is that what you think we were teaching you?"

"Of course!"

She shook her head. "Ror, your father and I—we wanted you to learn how to depend on yourself. Not be some street kid!"

"What about the King Kennedys? What were we then? Stealing electricity from the goddamn poles!" I shouted.

Ma got real quiet and still. She said, "We took what was ours, Ror, what had been stolen from us. We were fighting—the Vietnam War and Nixon's lies and the draft—we were fighting the greedy pigs who started that war so they could make money on the backs of our boys. We *could* fight—there was room for us. That was our—our *purpose*. Now, this country's changed. It scares me to think of all Reagan's done—money for the rich, nothing for us, as if we asked for this—then turning around and blaming it on us. Listen, Ror, I don't know how the world works anymore. If you get tangled up with the police, that means serious lawyers, and jail time, and I may not be able to help you. You don't want to mess up your life!"

"You've got to get that straight, Ror," Marilyn added.

"Are you saying I have nothing to fight against?" I asked. "Dado made his manifesto because he was sick of what the world forced on him! No wonder he was so paranoid. I watch TV. Look what it does! It makes me want—wish I had money to buy stuff I don't need. Makes me feel bad for who I really am. Every time I look in the mirror, I see it: I'm not like everyone else. Not even close!"

Ma's face shimmered pale. "Your father's plans didn't work out. You don't have to punish yourself for that."

"Graffiti's a way to take back what's mine!" I said.

"Dado went to the other extreme, Ror. *Nobody* could live the way he wanted!" Marilyn said.

"How would you know? You buy into that brand-name TV shit."

"So do you," she replied. "You were the first to break Number Seven with a Snickers bar. It doesn't make you any less human to want brand names."

She was right. I loved my Doc Martens boots and Gloria Vanderbilt jeans and my Design markers. I loved the feel of Krylon spray in my hand. I hated that I loved them.

"You could get killed doing graffiti, Ror," Marilyn went on. "Remember Michael Stewart, that guy the transit cops beat to shreds last year just for writing on a wall? He died. It scares me, what you do."

Talk about taking the gleam off my gold.

"Revolutionaries get killed. It happens," I said. "At least they're fighting for what they believe in."

Ma shook her head again. "You're not a revolutionary, Ror. You're just a kid. *My* kid."

"It's something I've got to do, Ma."

She kept shaking. "I can't let you."

"I've *got* to."

"Then I won't let you out of this house. We can stay here together. I'll give up the job search and teach you again," she said.

"No, I don't want that. I've come too far! You can't stop me!" I was shouting at her, just like kids and parents did all around us. "Oh, forget this!" I stood up from the table, grabbed my bag, and split.

30

I FELT LIKE a snail on a razor. Flesh inching forward on a sharp edge that split me in two.

Jonathan's was still open. I took my watercolor paintings out of my bag and stood outside his store, looking in. The thought of stealing that ebony black tightened my fingers around the paper he'd given me.

Why had I even come here?

I sifted through my paintings, looking at the likenesses of Dado, his patterns and configurations, his obsessiveness over gleaning and stripping and constructing that I'd been trying to recreate.

There were rich colors against hard lines when I added my ink pen; some were torn and layered in places. I was trying to work fast enough to avoid missing him, building with these

too-thin materials, trying to make them thick and dense and real. Trying to make the past real.

I opened the door and stepped in. Breathed in the fresh-cut wood smell of Dado's shop. I just wanted to be in Jon's store.

He saw me and stopped working and came out, stretching his back. I waited to be invited up, but when he didn't, I went to the counter and put my paintings down.

He came over, took the sheaf of paper, then looked at the first one. He was still for a long time before he turned to the next. And the next. He glanced at me, and back down.

"You've painted with watercolors before, I see," he said.

"I guess. I used to make my own out of pigments."

"Some unusual techniques here," he said.

"My dad taught me some stuff," I said.

"And where is your dad now?" he asked.

"He's dead."

Jonathan nodded like he knew. "So, Ror," he said. "You been getting into graffiti?"

My feet tried to find the ground. "How do you know?"

"Because I know those kids. Nessa, well—Nessa, that wild birdie. Trey Winthrop. He came to this neighborhood when he was thirteen, when his father got sick. He mighta got in Art and Design, if it wasn't for that."

"Trey told me his father left."

"Yeah?"

I shrugged.

"Kevin Battaglia. He tell you I gave him plenty of paper, enough to wrap around the earth? Reuben Gomez—I gave him painting lessons right here in my back room. I tried to help them all," he said. "But you—when you walked in here and I saw those drawings, Ror, I knew you were different. I thought you were a *really* good artist, that you had potential. But you steal from me again, I'm calling the police, I don't care who you are or where you came from or what you been through."

My face hot, I stared down at the paintings, colors swirling before my eyes. A rage burned in me.

How did a person know if they were any good, anyway?

He said, "Listen, you don't need those kids. You need to work seriously."

I met his milky eyes. Behind the anger, I saw he was— *invested*—like he cared if I came or went. Like he wasn't going to let me go so easily. *Why* did he care?

"You hear what I'm sayin' to you, Ror? Sometimes, you kids don't hear."

"I don't owe you anything," I said.

He stared at me hard. "You don't belong with any gang, either."

"They're not a gang!"

"I know—Noise Ink, Flying Skulls—you get messed up with them, you'll never get out."

I shook my head—he didn't know *anything* about them. "They're not a gang, dammit! They're a *crew*."

"You belong in a gallery, in a museum, Ror. Not a *crew!*"

The red fury I'd been holding in for months boiled over. "How do you know where I belong? What the hell is a museum— how does anybody even *get* into one? Or a *gallery*? I mean, who the hell wants to wait till they're dead to be seen when I can be seen every day on the street? Tell me that, old man!"

His face had that lost look, that surprise at my anger.

I pushed at him: "Well, what do you think? Where does someone like me go—*really* go? Who am I painting *for*? How do I know I'm any good? How do I know some gallery won't

ignore me like they did my Dado, huh? You work for them, you make these frames for them. How do I get in? I don't even have enough money to buy paint. So, what do I do, huh? Say something!"

I was sweating, breathing hard. My clothes felt too small. He was looking at me like from a high tower that was just getting higher, his belief in me winging further and further away. I didn't want to see that, but I couldn't help myself. "Trey says you have to be rich, white, know the right people. Or you have to be dead to get in those places. Forget it if you're a girl."

That flipped Jonathan. He gathered his breath and roared: "Trey! What the hell does *Trey* know? Open your eyes, for crissake, kiddo, get your head out of your ass and *go into* a gallery. There's plenty of living artists, and they're in galleries that anybody can go into, even someone like you, don't know her ass from her elbow. Walk down to Fifty-Seventh Street and look at Audrey Flack and think about what got her there. Go to SoHo. Go down the Village and look at young painters just coming up, like Keith Haring and Jean-Michel Basquiat—a homo and a black kid, for God's sake! Those guys *started* on the street, but they didn't *stay* there. Open your mind, Ror—I wouldn't be giving you supplies if I didn't think you were good enough. You need something, you ask me for it. You don't *steal* it. That makes you a petty thief, just like Trey." He banged his hand on the book. "Not an artist!"

I felt my mouth hanging, my breath sour in my dry throat. Like arguing with Dado in real life. I felt like an ass. I turned and ran.

It wasn't until I got home that I realized I'd left my paintings with him. No way I'd go back.

31

WAS JONATHAN RIGHT?

Was Ma? Marilyn?

Was Trey?

What did I feel, what did I really think—how come nobody asked me that?

It was a good thing, because I didn't have an answer.

32

I WAS SITTING in my room, drawing on the floor, when Dado came in with the roll of paper. He dumped it down and kicked it so it uncoiled. We watched as the path formed.

"Stand up, now, Ror," Dado said.

I did.

He reached to embrace me, and I could smell the chemical plant on him. I'd waited all day for him to come home. That sickly smell—I wished I could wash it from him.

"I'm so glad you came back, Dado," I said, hugging him hard. "I wanted to tell you, I got what you meant about saving me."

He held me gently by the shoulders so I could look deep into his husky-dog eyes. The last few years, he'd hardly met my gaze. Now, he let me in. I studied his dark widow's peak, his sharp nose. I hadn't seen him in so long.

"Come," he said, "I want to show you something."

We walked along the paper path as it opened up outside the dome. It was summertime, the acres a riot of flowers in bloom, the crickets chirping, the blue jays squawking, the bitter scent of the Kill floating over to us. I had that feeling I always did walking beside him—like together, he and I could enter into any realm. Like we lived now and in the past and in the future all at the same time. We existed at any and every moment together. As we walked, I thought—I don't know anything about your insides, or why you took your own life, but I know I love you, and that's the best I can do right now. That's all I ever could do for you.

We passed through the Island, and over the bay somehow, into Manhattan. Together, we went into a gallery showing a painter whose work I didn't know. Words written all over the walls, over faces whose open mouths were filled with letters, forced to eat them, the paint so fresh, it almost looked wet. The work made us gasp—we turned to each other.

Dado started laughing.

"Who is it by?" I asked. I looked around for a name.

He took out a bottle and stuffed in a rag, making a Molotov cocktail.

"I'm going to save you from me," he said. "Or you will never get here."

He lit the rag and threw the bottle into the room. It crashed and burst into flame. I tried to scream, but nothing would come out. I felt the heat and agonized over the melting paintings. He stepped into the wild fire—

The sound of laughter woke me. I opened my eyes, blinking, blinking, my breath exploding into my lungs. I listened to my sister's snores, Ma asleep on the couch. She had let me back in. The TV's glow lit up our one room: knotted dream catchers over stained carpet, used couch, half-fridge filled with food-stamp food. Clothes in boxes. Even Marilyn had given up trying to keep it neat. *One day,* I said to myself, *one day, I'm going to get us the hell out of here.*

In the hall, I heard light, familiar footsteps dancing down the stairs. I jumped off the top bunk quiet as a gazelle and pulled on my jeans, hurrying in my bare feet.

At the bottom floor of our building, I caught up to him.

"Trey! Where you going?"

"Hey, what you doing up?"

"I had an awful nightmare." I rubbed my face with both hands. "Then I heard you."

He chewed on his bottom lip, clearly thinking about what to tell me. "Get your shoes on," he finally said. "I'll wait."

I snuck back into our apartment, laced on my boots, threw on a bra and sweatshirt and snagged my backpack. Quietly, I locked up after myself. Trey waited outside.

WE WALKED HALF a block west, my head still in the dream, before I asked Trey, "Where are we going?"

"Check out the trains."

"What for?"

"To see what we see," he said.

I struggled against the craving to throw my arms around him, to just stop and bury my face in his neck until the bad dream faded. I walked a little behind him, his long stride always getting ahead.

"Hey, Trey?"

"'Sup?"

"Am I doing it all wrong with the crew?"

He slowed his steps. "We got a lot of water under the bridge, you know? Been together a long time. Ain't so easy to fit you in, R."

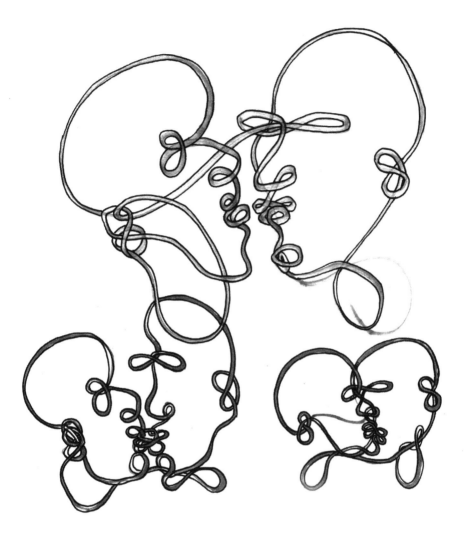

Now I wanted it more than ever.

As if he read my mind, he said, "Just, we got business to work out. We got other crews after us. Noise Ink, we strange enough already without another girl." His hair was tied back in a ponytail puff, showing his high forehead. He looked softer without a hat. We turned on Broadway. "What was your nightmare?" he asked.

"My daddy-o," I said.

Trey seemed curious. "What about him?"

"He brought me a roll of paper, and he kicked it out like he wanted to show me something, and we went on this long trip, and ended up in a gallery, and I don't know why I'm telling you this. I don't like to talk about it."

"You're telling me 'cause I'm asking," Trey said. He stopped and turned to me for the first time. Did he have his own father nightmares? Jonathan said his father got sick. Was that why he left? "So?"

I hit myself in the heart with a closed fist. "You ever feel like you're so numb, you could stab yourself and not even know the knife went through?"

He stuck his hand in his front pocket, and I noticed his jeans, button-up Levi's, tight in all the right places. "Yeah, like my little brother, James. He's gonna be three. Since our daddy's gone, he's been banging his head on the door like he's tryin' to get out. Just won't stop sometimes."

I looked down at the sidewalk, not sure what to say.

Trey said, "Why'd your pops bring you the paper?"

"It was like he put me on a path, the way it rolled out," I said. I looked at him. "You think maybe you'd want to go to a gallery with me sometime?"

He held my look for a long moment, something going on in his head he wasn't saying. "What gallery?"

"I don't know. Jonathan said I should go."

"Jonathan?"

A car swished by. I knew from Trey's face I was on shaky ground. I pressed on. "From the store."

Trey's eyes narrowed. "You talkin' to Jonathan?"

"He said he tried to help you. While your daddy was sick."

We stared at each other until Trey looked away, out into the empty street. "A lot went down. He ain't a black man. Not everybody gets the same chance."

"Not everybody's good as you. He told me about this artist, said he was a black kid. Coming up. In some gallery. You want to go see him?"

Trey darted his hand out, reached for my chin. "I like your face, you know that?" he said, holding my jaw.

I didn't say anything about him changing the subject. "I like yours, too." I grazed his cheek with my fingertips. It was softer than I expected.

"You sure you don't want me?" he said with a little smile.

"I didn't mean that."

He dropped his hand and grasped mine. "You should let me draw you again. This time, for real," he said, squeezing my fingers. He let go, turned, and started walking. We got to the subway, and he led the way down the steps.

34

WE WALKED TO the rear end of the platform, and there, sitting on the bench in front of the Fire Pops Trey had painted were Nessa, Reuben, and Kevin. My heart seized all the way to my feet. When she saw us, Nessa's face went slack. She stood up quickly, took a couple of steps, and said, "Lookee what the cat drug in."

"Hey, Ror," Reuben said in a wary tone.

Kevin held his hand out for a slap as he said to Trey, "You didn't say nothing about her coming. This is a secret mission. She ain't even in the crew yet."

That hurt.

Trey nodded, glancing at me. "Yeah, I just ran into her."

Nessa stood close to me and looked up, forcing me to look down at her. I hadn't realized how short she was. How she combed her perfect eyebrows straight up, like she was trying to be Brooke Shields.

"I couldn't sleep," I said. "I heard Trey going down the steps in our building. He let me tag along."

She lifted her chin like she didn't believe me and turned to him. He didn't meet her eyes. Goddamn, why did I have that tearing inside? Not cool to like her boyfriend so much. Too close to trouble.

Then Trey clapped his hands. "You guys ready?"

"She's coming?" Nessa asked.

"Coming where?" I asked.

Trey turned on her. "Yo, I thought you said it was all right, another girl!"

"Yeah, but—"

"So, just—"

Kevin interrupted, waggling his long fingers. "Look, let's just go." He got up from the bench. "Before the blue boys come."

Go where? As he started to walk away, I saw he had a huge backpack but no skateboard. Reuben carried a pack, too. Nessa wasn't wearing her headphones, was dressed in saggy sweats. Trey without any hat. Kevin walked to the end of the platform and went down the steps, into the tunnel, Reuben and Nessa right after. Zings of fear struck my heart, cold down to my stomach. Where the hell were they going? Should I just go home? I glanced at Trey, and he nodded, *Get moving.* I followed them to the edge, and froze, with Trey behind me.

Wait. This wasn't what I'd thought. Trains came speeding out of that tunnel; they could flatten you in a second. The third rail could zap you. Rats could eat off your face. I stared down into the garbage puddle in the middle of the rusty track, the stairs trailing off into the darkness. And I thought *trains* were bad—no way I was going down there.

Trey muttered, "You want to be one of us? Don't just stand there, move it!"

A push from behind got my feet going. He nudged me along, down the stairs, into total darkness, not giving my eyes a chance to adjust. I could hear Kevin and Reuben ranking on me somewhere up ahead—

"Ror's so scared, I think she's gonna shit a perfect brick."

"No, no, she's so scared, we're gonna have to break her legs to keep her movin'."

"We disruptin' her shitty reality, awright."

I smelled sewage and Nessa's sweet, gummy perfume close by and felt Trey still behind me, the tracks under my feet, the bumps of every tie in between. My eyes were starting to see as we stumbled from column to column. Sick, dark fear controlled me. I thought of R. Crumb's *Keep on Truckin'*, and it was the only way I kept going.

"How do we know when a train's coming?" I asked.

"We don't," Nessa said.

"They could rush by and cut your feet off," Reuben said.

"Then you be walking around on stumps." She laughed.

"Yo, they could cut your head off," Trey said. His fingers brushed the back of my neck, sending shivers through me.

"They could flatten you any second," Reuben said.

I thought I might throw up right there.

I held my hands in front of me, and they caught on Nessa's sweatshirt. She sucked her teeth and pushed them away, saying, "Get a grip." I felt warm fingers on my neck, directing me to the side. Trey.

Suddenly, out of the dark, an express train came flying by on the center track, big, hard, metal, kicking up dirt and dust, filling my eyes with grit. I screamed and screamed, wanting to run back, or forward, to safety. No one could hear me. I stopped screaming and stood still, hands over my ears until it passed. I felt Trey's fingers shaking as he let go of my neck.

After it went by, we moved on.

"Fuck, will someone just tell me where we're going?" I said, pissed.

"Top secret. We'd have to kill you if we told you," Kevin said from somewhere up there, his tall pinhead under a golden light. Weaving behind him, Reuben, with his long hair I suddenly wanted to pull.

"We're going to get killed, is no one but me worried about that?" I thought of Ma and Marilyn, what they said. Damn, this was stupid. Jonathan was right. I was better than this; I didn't have to do it this way.

"Stop complaining and keep going," Nessa muttered.

I thought of death. We could die here and no one would

find us. I thought of Kevin's name, NIL, and I wondered if he had any special philosophy about dying while you're already underground.

"Train!" Reuben shouted, and we hid behind the columns. This one came slower, and I could see the people on it. Night workers. They knew where they were headed—I wished I did. I wished I could control the sweat soaking my upper lip and my pits.

When the train had passed, Kevin darted across the tracks and headed down a different tunnel along a curve. The tunnel led zigzag, this way and that; I could hear trains going by far away, even above me. I got the feeling I could walk along these tracks for weeks and never surface. Lost and never found. Trains went into boroughs like worms through a dead man's eyes. There must be hundreds of miles of track.

Just ahead, I saw lights. Dim lights at the end of the tunnel, not bright enough for a station. A way out; I started breathing again. Kevin and Reuben broke and ran ahead. Nessa kept walking steady, taking the lead. We came to what looked like a secret station—train after train parked along the platforms, all numbers 1 and 2 and 3. I jumped up onto the platform after Nessa, and resisted the urge to lay myself down and kiss the ground.

Just then, Kevin and Reuben came back carrying shopping bags they dumped down. All of them were full of spray cans.

Reuben said, "Jackpot!"

Kevin explained, "They left the stash right where you said, Trey."

"That fuckin' Frankie gets dumber every day," Trey said.

35

NESSA KNELT AND took cans out of the bags, standing them up and twirling them around to read their labels. "Check this. None of it's Rusto or Krylon. It's the wack Red Devil shit you get at Woolworth's."

Woolworth's? They sold spray paint at the nickel-and-dime store?

Reuben took off his backpack, looking down at the cans. "Some of these colors are good."

Kevin said, "At least we don't have to use our own shit."

They got down with Nessa, picking out cans. Reuben carefully gathered eight in his arms and headed down to the last car. Kevin took almost as many and went after him. Nessa and Trey picked theirs. Six cans were left. I sat next to them.

Train doors opened between cars, somebody lit a cigarette,

someone else passed a joint, the *ssssst* of beer tops popped. The *rattle rattle* of cans, the sounds of laughing and joking.

Baby blue. Hot pink.

Terra-cotta. Indian spice.

Turtle. Yellowburst.

I lined the cans up, feeling their weight. I held one in each hand, then switched them. I kept thinking someone was going to take them away from me.

I didn't know what to paint. I didn't want to just spray. It was one thing to sell comix to kids, or paint in an abandoned building or on an out-of-the-way park wall, but this was the subway. *Millions* of people would see. Like the Fire Pops Trey did in the station. My audience would be the city. My sister. Ma. And whenever I learned a new tool, I had to use it over and over until I got it in my system, until it became part of my muscles and I could use it without thinking. I had only sprayed a few times, not enough to be any good. Here, in this sublevel of the soul, I couldn't make any mistakes. My first shot had to be perfect.

I opened my pad, flipping through drawings to find just the right one for the train. My dream haunted me, those destroyed faces with words floating from their lips. The words. They were lines of TV bullshit that had gotten stuck in my system and ate at the edges of my consciousness. I could spray them across this train, give them back to the world my way.

Trey called out to me, "Yo, Ror, what you doin', man?"

TIME TO MAKE THE DONUTS   HEY, KID!
WE DO CHICKEN RIGHT
HEY, KID ! YOU KNOW WHAT YOU LIKE
        IT'S THE REAL THING
REAGAN SAYS : HOMELESS WANT TO BE HOMELESS
RAY-GUN
              YOU JUST CAN'T HELP THEM ! !

I looked up; he had already outlined half his name. He was painting a whole car! I couldn't find the place in me that would get up and spray. I could only sit and draw.

"We ain't got all night," he said. "Get your ass movin'."

"I don't know what to do," I said.

He came over and took a look. "What's all that?"

"I don't know."

He said, "Come on. Pick a car, pick a car. Get to it, baby. You ain't writing a fuckin' jingle."

I felt Nessa over there, watching.

Trey grabbed my can of pink and threw it at me. I caught it. "Get up. Paint a fuckin' octopus, don't matter, just do it."

I got up and went to the train behind me, shaking the can. *An octopus.*

"Not there." He came over and ran his finger down the bumpy side. "This is a ridgie. It's hard to paint. Do it here." He pointed to the train everyone else was painting, a smooth one. "You thinkin' too much. Just do your tag." He walked away, back to his own painting.

I went to the big spot between Reuben and Kevin, and froze. Tag. Octopus. *It's the real thing.*

"Just fuckin' paint already, home skillet!" Trey shouted over to me.

As high as I could reach, I started. The first spray seemed to go inside me, like a shot of pink electricity, waking me from my stupor. *I'm spraying on a train.* Like a hallucination that was so real, it was true. The bitter smell stirred me, the splatter force close to the car as I outlined a letter A. *I'm doing it!* I tried to keep up with the speed of the spray, the size of my metal canvas. I stepped back, replaced pink for green and sprayed out U, then got stuck, not sure how to space the letters, how much room to take. I watched the crew. They all had their own ways of doing things.

Kevin was like this:

Trey was like this:

Nessa was like this:

Reuben was like this:

Me, I think I looked like this:

I tried to control it, to measure it, the dimensions of the letters, but it all seemed to go out of control so fast, to get sloppy in my hands. I needed more practice; I didn't know how to do this, to handle these cans and colors. I stepped back after each letter. Compared to what the crew was doing, my AURA didn't stand out. Even though it was four colors, it looked gray dull to me. Bad. One note.

I called out to Kevin next to me, "Hey, why we doin' this?"

He took a swig of beer. "I don't know 'bout you, but I wanna be king." He raised the can in a toast to his painting. "That's me. Top Dawg. You get up in every train line in the city, you're famous. Everybody'll look at NIL and say, 'Man, I just saw him inna Bronx, in Brooklyn. Up and down and all over town. He's the shit.'"

I was stunned. "Every train line in the city?"

He nodded. "Ride the rails and hit up all the train lines, and everybody'll know your name. Get it?"

"So you have to go through these tunnels all the time?"

He nodded. As he got back to work, he seemed to transform into the Ninja of Spray, his every move a confident chop of the can carving out his name on the train. "The more you get up, the more crews see you and know your name. Them's the rules."

Suddenly, all I wanted to do was paint an amazing fucking octopus sucking up New York City on the side of this one train car, spitting words out the ends of its suction cups. "What if I don't follow the rules, exactly?"

He sprayed a long line of red. "If you can't even do the rules, then you just a toy." I stared at my disappointing AURA. He said, "Yo, Ror, think of all the stuffed shirts commuting home, looking at the boring ads on the platform, and here you come on the side of the train, *Pow!*"

I looked at my word. *Pow.*

"You'll open up their sleepy eyes. Give them some dream to chew on. You'll make their fuckin' day!"

Now I really wanted to paint my octopus with every detail I could muster. Disrupt their shitty reality.

"You got any caps that'll spray skinny lines?" I asked him.

He dug through his pockets and handed me a few.

Surrounding my AURA, starting from the end of Reuben's outlined O to the beginning of Kevin's N, I sprayed up over the windows a drawing that came easier to me than the letters—a living breathing swirling screaming hot pink terra-cotta baby blue yellowburst octopus that took over the city and everyone in it, even the roaches that didn't want to be my friends.

When it was done, I stepped back and said, "POW!"

36

TREY'S PIECE TOOK up an entire car and would blow anybody's mind, even the blue boys', even Jonathan's, even the Pope's. Looking at it, I saw why he was Roi. King. I suddenly got his joke on my Fire Pops now—Kings. The King of Pop, Michael Jackson; the King of Comedy, Richard Pryor; their heads on fire with the genius of their work, burning the candle at both ends, close to a flame that almost killed them.

Trey was King of the Underground. He was on fire.

I saw him staring at my piece, blinking kind of fast. Did he think it was any good? The way the giant octopus ate the AURA, it wasn't exactly like the other tags. The guys started joking about it:

"That's cold, Ror—you be watching too many late-night movies."

"You got a baaaaad aura, making that squid barf like that."

Trey took a camera out of his bag and turned it on me in front of my painting. *Flash.* Nessa glared like she wanted to spray over me, like they did with that Frankie guy. Trey snapped a few more pics, then walked over to TNT (*gonna take you out*) with her big-haired girl and flashed one of her. He took one of NIL (*God is dead*) and ME ONE (*me too*). He took some of his own piece, then he said, "Let's blow this joint."

We threw the empty spray cans under the platform and went back through the tunnel, holding our ears and stopping to let trains go by. I didn't want to leave my painting down there after working on it for so long. The farther I got from it, the more I felt I was losing it all over again. Like in the fire. As we walked, I asked Trey, "Ever feel like you want to do something you can take with you?"

He shook his head. "Can't take nothin' with you anyways, in the end. Tomorrow, we'll go after school, then you'll see. Eyes checking out your piece." He pointed to his eyes with two fingers, then to mine.

"The eyes, right," I said. Millions of eyes looking at my aura.

We left the crew and went to the hotel. Upstairs, he held his hand out, and I slipped my fingers inside his. He added a hug at the end, our hands still between us. I held him to me and breathed him in—spray, smoke, beer. He whispered in my ear, "I know you were scared tonight." He kissed the side of my head, said, "Still think you better than me?" and laughed and ran up his stairs by twos.

I smiled big as hell and took a few deep breaths and unlocked the door as quietly as I could. The TV was off, Ma on the couch, Marilyn in bed. I listened for Ma's sleeping breath as I slipped out of my pants, and climbed to the top bunk. The whole world screamed in my head, the night spray, the wild colors, the sounds of cans rattling, the smell of paint, Trey.

I couldn't wait until tomorrow.

37

I BUMPED INTO Nessa in the school bathroom. I watched her put on her bubble-gum lipstick. She held it up and caught my eye in the mirror. "You want some?" she asked. I fixed my cap and looked at my face and saw Trey's painting of me—lips full and plain. Bangs down over one dark-circled green eye.

I shook my head. "No thanks."

"You could be pretty, Ror. I think Reuben likes you," she said.

"Hmm," I said. When I closed my eyes and wished for a boy, it wasn't Reuben.

She rolled down the lipstick, covered it, threw it back in her bag. She was just trying to distract me from Trey. I thought of how Reuben had finally warmed to me, joked with me, slapped my hand in the hall that morning. Was it possible? Could I feel anything for him?

In art, Trey sat down and said, "Check it, five o'clock,

we meet, go down the station right at the start of rush hour. Then you'll see what I'm talkin' 'bout. People hooked on our cars." He rubbed his hands together. "They won't be able to stop lookin'!"

"How do we know our train will pull in then?"

"Reuben's uncle works for the TA. That's where he lifted the keys to open the train doors and got the schedules and shit."

"How will—I mean, will people know it's us?"

"Crews will. You'll see, R, just chill."

But I couldn't think about anything else for the rest of the day except those millions of eyes on my brain-sucking octopus. All New York would look at my painting and come alive. Their lives would stop for that moment, and the picture would flash before them, and it would burn a hole in their minds forever. Wake them up.

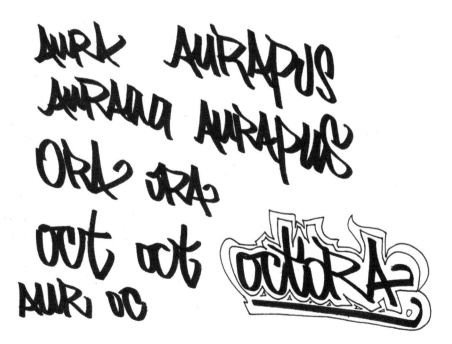

After school, I ran home, told the drunk to get lost, and locked myself in the bathroom for a lukewarm shower. I got into my black jeans and my Hendrix T-shirt, laced up my boots, put on the new red cap Ma made me.

I waited outside for Trey. Reuben walked up the street with Nessa, Kevin bumped onto the curb with his board. Finally, Trey came out in his fishing hat.

Heat rose from the evening sidewalks; clammy people with suit jackets slung over their shoulders jumbled out of the subway entrance. We pushed our way down the funk-smelling stairs, pulled back the turnstiles and slipped through, and jockeyed to the rear of the station against the flow of traffic. Trey slid into the one open space on the bench; Nessa plopped onto his lap and started kissing him, and he let her. I looked away. Reuben pulled stickers out of his pocket and slapped them onto the wall behind me, making a pattern of small green aliens. I asked him for a sticker, and he gave me one. I looked into his smooth face for scars, something I could latch on to, something that would tell me how deep he went. Something else to think about instead of the smooching beside me.

"Where do you get these?" I asked.

"The post office over on Broadway and Eighty-Ninth."

Loud wet kisses. I tried to focus on Reuben, ignoring the churning in my stomach.

"Come with me next time, we'll pick up a bunch," he said. "We can hang out at my place and draw them in."

"Uh, yeah, sure, right," I mumbled.

Trey extracted himself from Nessa, saying, "You're gonna make me miss it." We turned to each other at the same time, then he cast his eyes on the tracks. He pushed Nessa off his lap and stood up. A train came into the station, dumped people, took them on and left. It wasn't ours.

I went over and stood next to him on the edge of the platform, gazing down the tunnel I'd walked through last night, willing the train to come. Another pulled into the station. Not ours.

"Shit, man, when's it gonna be here?" I asked Trey, leaning against the column beside him.

"Patience, Grasshopper." He took out a marker and tagged his name quick as breathing.

Two headlights wiggled toward us—on the front, I saw it—NOISE INK. I cried, "That's it!"

In the crowd, Trey slipped his hand in mine and gave it a squeeze before he let go. People crammed their way to the edge, impatient for the train to stop. At the other column, Reuben and Kevin hung on, their heads turned, waiting. Nessa stood on her tiptoes behind us, her breath on my neck.

The train pulled in layered with tags, and I saw ours— first Trey's, then Nessa's, then the car with mine and Kevin's and Reuben's—and I gasped. In the fluorescents of the station, it stood out in neon-bright colors like Times Fucking Square. It was dazzling, like fireworks in a night sky; no one

could deny the hard metal solidness of it. Jubilant, I peered at the waiting crowd on the platform, eager to see the recognition, those alive eyes Trey and Kevin talked so much about.

But.

Everyone just wanted to get home. Their annoyed eyes didn't give a shit. They didn't see the colors shining in their brainwashed faces.

They had no clue we had worked so hard for them. I looked over at Trey, who stared like he'd hoped for something different. Like this wasn't the way it usually went.

The train doors opened. People bulldozed their way off. Others crammed on. The doors closed. The train rumbled out, taking my painting with it. The station drained of people. I stood there feeling like somebody punched the wind out of me. The crew clung to the columns, no one saying anything. I swallowed the pride dust stuck in my throat.

"Looking good, man. The boys inna Bronx are gonna shit when they see it," Reuben finally said.

I could tell he was waiting for me to say something, too. Did I care about the boys in the Bronx? They seemed to.

"That was a fuckin' burner, Trey," Kevin said.

"Yeah," Reuben agreed.

Trey nodded, half looking at me.

People started filling the platform again.

"Well, I gotta go," Reuben said. He peeled off and walked away.

"Yeah, me too."

"See ya."

We drifted down the station like directionless clouds on a windless day.

38

MR. GARCI WHEELED a giant TV-video hookup into art class to play us an episode of Andy Warhol's cable show, but he couldn't get the equipment to work. A geek tried to plug the red to the red, the black to the black, or whatever, but there was no picture. Kids started getting restless, drawing on desks, their hands, each other, until Garci said, "Okay, folks, let's put that aside," and I couldn't tell you how disappointed I was.

My Warhol had burned in the fire, but here in the city he showed up like a new penny in the *Village Voice*, the *Arts Weekly*, the gossip columns about clubs and parties, everywhere someone needed a reminder of the outer limits. Doing graf, I felt far from him. Under my pillow, I kept an *Interview* magazine I found in the trash. I still loved to look at what he did.

"I'm sure you all know the artist Andy Warhol—considered

the King of Pop Art," Mr. Garci said, "though there are those who would disagree."

Did Michael Jackson get "King of Pop" from Andy Warhol?

I looked over at Trey in his Sherlock Holmes hat, a little smile dangling on his face.

Garci went through Andy's history—his illustrations, his films, his silkscreens of famous movie stars and car crashes, his collaborations, his Factory. He suddenly seemed to me like a man who strapped drums to his chest, cymbals between his knees, a harmonica at his mouth, an accordion in his hands. A one-man band who played everything, or at least tried it out.

"Warhol is all about selling himself," Mr. Garci went on,

"and I say that with no criticism intended." *That's why Dado hated him*, I realized. "He's an artist who knows how to *use* the attention on himself; he doesn't let *it* use *him*. That's something all artists could learn."

"Yo, I know how to sell myself, Mr. G," Trey said, with a wink to me.

"That's good, Mr. T, because right now, I want you all to think of an advertisement for yourself. Before we get into making our silkscreen stencils, take this chance to let the world know who you are. What would you say?"

Kids called out:

"Best sex on the Upper West Side."

"Eats ten hot dogs an hour."

"Hottest—no—*smartest* chick in the projects."

"Just Say Yes!"

I glanced over at Trey, who hung his fingers in his armpits, watching everybody. He mouthed to me, "King of the Underground."

He knew who he was.

Garci put up his hands and laughed. "Okay, now, take your commercial—"

"Hey, Mr. Garci, isn't this like the opposite of those anti-artists who were, like, anti-commerce?" Sarah asked.

"Yes—very good, excellent, Sarah! Warhol is the opposing force of Dada, yes. Now, try to boil your commercial down to one symbol. Like yin-yang, or the hammer and sickle. What would your symbol be? That's your stencil."

He passed out cardstock and I fingered it, thinking of my Bad Barbies, my Fire Pop, my AURA under the reaching, suctioning tentacles of an octopus. In a flash, I saw it: If I made a stencil, I could use it over and over—a stencil was like a print, a stamp, a brand. Like Levi's, like Coke, like Tampax, like Band-Aids. Now I drew out the octopus and put Ronald Reagan's head coming from underneath, saying his lies about people like me, people with no homes and no jobs. I busted them open like shelling peanuts. I was a lie-busting octopus. I'd make him eat his words. I was Octora.

Trey was drawing a crown made from a top hat. *Roi.*

"Hey," I said to him, "why don't we do this stencil thing with spray? We could just cut the outline of anything we want,

then go out real quick, and zip, zip, paint on the street!" I'd seen that; people did that; I liked the way it looked.

He pressed his lips and squinted, shaking his head. "That won't fly."

"Says who?"

"Man, if Frankie gets the word out—'Trey don't do his own paintings, he uses a stencil'—I'm shit. That lardbucket's just lookin' for any way to fuck up my rep."

"Why are you *so* obsessed with Frankie, Trey?" I asked.

He glanced at Garci nearby. "Not here. After school, outside, I'll tell you."

I knew he didn't like it, but I couldn't let go of the stencil idea. It made a whole lot of sense to me—you could take all the time you wanted with the drawing at home, cut it out, and when you went into the world to spray, it would be fast and clean. I didn't really care much what some lardbucket named Frankie thought of that.

39

SITTING IN THE SUNSHINE outside school waiting for Trey, I watched kids flirt by hitting each other or howling like wolves and yanking at backpacks. I could feel it rising, what this early June promised, the coming summer freedom like a hot, honey liquid that threatened to spill from me. I took off my pack, rolled my cap up on my forehead and the sleeves of my T-shirt over my shoulders.

Trey hopped down the steps toward me and held out his hand for a slap. He said, "How do you get rid of an asshole?"

I knew he was talking about Frankie. "I don't know. Steal his shit?"

"We got a plan of action," Trey said.

"What is it?"

"Can you dance?" he asked.

I thought of concerts, of nights in front of the fires. "Damn straight. I dance like an animal spirit. Like a gypsy queen." I did a few moves with my hands and shoulders.

Trey pushed his hat back and eyed me up and down. He nodded and smiled. "Yeah, boyee, I bet you go buck wild. Listen, next Friday, our crew and Poison Crew, we're gonna have a dance, like B-boys breakin' it on the street—only wild style, a cypher with all-city crews jammin' it. End this shit once and for all. Best man standing wins. The others walk away. We don't bother each other again."

"You ever going to tell me what happened with you and Frankie, how all this got started?"

Trey wouldn't meet my eyes. "He thinks he's hot shit on a silver platter because he goes to Art and Design, but he's just cold diarrhea on a paper plate—Oh, fuck!"

"What?"

"There he is."

I followed the line of Trey's eyes down the street to a tall flame-haired guy as built as a football player, dressed in a camo T-shirt with fatigues and combat boots, flanked by a bruiser on either side. I felt Trey pull himself up to his full height. I couldn't stop looking at Frankie, the way he walked up the block like he owned it. He was at least a head taller than Trey. Kids scootched away from him. He really didn't give a shit what anyone thought. My stomach dipped; I kept my distance from guys like him, and here he was coming right for us.

He went up in Trey's face and said in a quiet, hoarse voice, "What's with the hat, fool? You some kind of Sherlock Homey?"

"Don't make me go off on you, Frankie," Trey said, his voice steady. "This ain't the time or the place. We got the cypher next week, and the whole fuckin' city will decide who's better, you or us, once 'n' for all, so shut the fuck up."

Frankie turned his head slowly to look at me. It felt like his brown eyes knew me in a way that scared me down deep. "This your hot new Octopussy here?" He reached out and plucked off my cap and threw it down, screaming, "*You stealing my shit, Octopussy?*"

I covered my head with my hands.

"Back off, Frankie, you on my ground!" Trey warned.

Frankie pushed him. "You got another ho doing all your dirty work now?"

"The cypher gonna end this—"

"*Stay outta my shit!*" Frankie cried. He hauled off and punched Trey in the chest, but Trey jumped away before the fist hit him too hard. People started to watch. Trey whacked Frankie, who lumbered at him, tried to catch him. Trey was too fast. Kids made a circle around us, jostling closer to see. One of his boys shoved me, and I stumbled back and fell through the crowd, hard on my ass, the sidewalk scraping my palms. Outrage boiled in me. I felt for my knife; no knife.

Trey shouted, "Goddamn, Frankie, you asshole, yo mama so fuckin' ugly, she make an onion cry!"

Everyone jeered and howled. I heard flesh hitting flesh, grunts.

"Fuck you, you fuck! Don't talk about my mother like that!"

Hoots went up from the circle. I found my way to my feet.

Frankie got in a punch. Trey shrieked, "Yo mama so stank, her teeth duck when she yawns!"

Screams of laughter.

"I'ma kill you!" Frankie went after him harder. In a flash, out of nowhere, Nessa charged in, her nails scratching Frankie's face. Reuben and Kevin rushed behind her. I got in and threw myself at the guy on Trey, pulling him backward, off balance. The guy elbowed me so hard in the stomach I couldn't breathe. I felt fists on my back and someone yanked at my T-shirt and knocked me in the face, and my ears started ringing.

Trey whooped, "We gonna make this battle real! You better watch your ass!"

Metallic blood filled my mouth. I heard voices: "Break it up, kids, break it up. Let's get moving." Hands on my arms separated me from the fight. I tried to catch my breath as teachers waded into the middle of the brouhaha, braying at people to step off.

Mr. Garci went for Kevin and Reuben, and I never saw him so mad, his face beet red with fury.

The principal grabbed Trey and forced his elbows behind him like a cop would.

Two gym teachers started hustling Frankie and his boys on down the street.

"You ain't gonna win this war," Kevin yelled. "We ain't done yet!"

One of theirs yelled back, "We'll kick your asses!"

"Come on, come on." The principal took Trey and Nessa inside by the scruffs of their necks. Garci disappeared with Kevin and Reuben. The crowd, hyped by adrenaline, their sap risen to the top, laughed like they just saw gladiators. I stood dazed, my ears buzzing, sucking the blood back into my mouth, feeling like I got hit by a truck.

I heard a familiar voice behind me.

"Hey, little sister. Hey, what happened? You okay?" I turned to see Marilyn holding up my cap. She took out a tissue and gave it to me. I pressed the red into it. She put my cap

back on my head and brushed off my face, pushing aside my bangs and looking into my eyes, her skin gone ghostly. "What the hell was *that* all about?" she asked.

How could I explain to her about the crews, Trey, the paint? Especially when I couldn't explain it to myself.

"I don't know," I said.

She narrowed her eyes like she didn't believe me. "All right, fine, I care about you, okay? So just tell me, I won't judge you, promise."

I looked down at myself: dirty, my T-shirt torn at the neck.

"Don't you have finals to study for or something?" I asked. She usually stayed after school with some group or other before she had to go to work.

She flicked something off my shoulder. "No, no. Let's go home and clean you up." I wiped sweat away, and we started walking. She said, "You think I'm going to rat you out to Ma, is that it? Listen, Ror, I tell her things because I'm afraid for you. What if you saw me, I don't know, shooting up or something? Wouldn't you tell her?"

I glanced at my sister's glam makeup, at her big-sprayed hair. Is that what she thought, graffiti was like shooting up heroin? I shook my head. "What I do is nothing like *that*," I said.

"It's just, when you act crazy, I worry about you."

Crazy. The word she always used for Dado. "I'm not crazy. I know what I'm doing." My voice was ice.

"You're going to destroy yourself, Rora."

I stopped walking. "Do I get this hassle *all* the way home?"

She looked at me hard. Sometimes, I wished I had her brain, the way she cut through all the self-questioning and doubt and got right to normal. She did well in school, she worked, she had friends. But it wasn't like that for me. She sighed and shook her head and made a zip across her lips, like *No more mention of graffiti.*

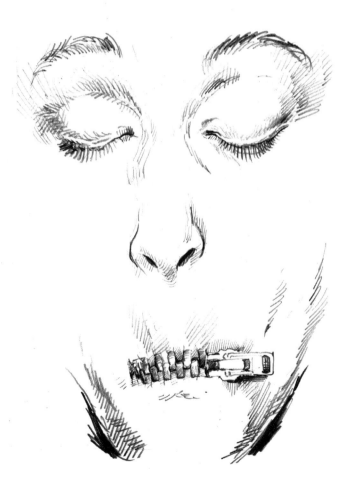

40

MARILYN WAS HOLDING ice to my lip when Ma came in with her selling suitcase and leaned it carefully against the wall, all the while watching us.

For once, Marilyn didn't speak for me.

After a moment, I said, "I got mixed up in something." It hurt to talk.

"I see that," Ma said, fear simmering beneath her anger. "And what am I supposed to think?"

In my head, I heard Dado's burr-edged voice singing his Blake poetry:

Helpless, naked, piping loud
like a fiend hid in a cloud

"It was art, wasn't it?" I realized as I spoke. "That's what happened to Dado."

She came closer, sat at the table with us. She said, "It's not so black-and-white."

"They didn't accept him. He never found his place."

"*He* didn't fit in anywhere, Ror, but he thought *you* would." Ma said.

My ears started ringing again, my face got warm. "He did?"

She spoke in a rush, like she'd been thinking about it, just waiting for me to ask. "There was like a—a special room inside him where only you could go, a kind of magical aurora borealis with colored lights in a night sky. He named you, he saw it in you from the moment you were born, Ror. The way he talked about you—he thought you could be what he wasn't. He believed in you."

Marilyn took a sharp breath, as if Dado's belief in me annoyed her.

But that belief weighed a thousand pounds, pressure like a vise grip squeezing me in a direction I couldn't go. I thought of movements—Pop, Surrealism, Dada, how Dado moved me backward in time, to the classic, to what came before. But I was trying to go forward.

"The manifesto," I said. "He was trying to make rules. Rules that fit him."

Ma tapped on the table and sighed. "The manifesto was a map so he wouldn't get lost. Only the rules got all confused in his head. They took on a life of their own."

"That manifesto didn't make any sense," Marilyn said. We both looked at her. "It was full of contradictions. 'We will not let ambition cloud our love. We must fight for what we want and win. We won't trust anyone. We won't need anyone. Nothing is free, including love. Love is our connection to earth, the reason why we're here.' Bullshit, all of it. I wanted to scream at him—'How can you love without trust, Daddy? How can you fight for what you want and win—without ambition?' It just doesn't make sense."

At the center of my life was the last thing he said to me— *I'm going to save you, girl.* What he did destroyed everything we knew and came close to destroying us. That was the biggest contradiction of all.

Yet I understood it.

I understood *him.*

He knew we'd get out, and we did. If he hadn't burned the whole thing to the ground—burned *himself* to the ground—I would've been stuck inside that four-acre madness on Staten Island with him forever. Marilyn would have escaped, but not me. Since we came here, I felt my world open up. I was in the middle of a city full of art. I'd met Trey, Jonathan, Mr. Garci, the boys, even Nessa. Somehow, this was the only way Dado had known to save me from his own fate.

Was that it?

In the silence, Ma got up and put some water in a pot to boil. It would be rice or pasta for dinner again. "Girls," she finally said, turning to us, "it's been hard, but we have to move on. We have to pull ourselves together. Next week is the meeting about the property." Marilyn and I looked at each other. "Mr. Jones—he's a tough lawyer who thinks he can build a solid case—he thinks the three of us have a good chance of proving we homesteaded with your father for fifteen years and can claim possession. If we do prove it, we can sell the land and pay him off and get out of here. He's already tracked down Randy, who got him in touch with Krishna. He's looking for everyone else. He's taking statements, and he needs ours, too. He says he needs both of you there to give your history."

"I wouldn't miss it for the world," Marilyn said, looking at me to make sure I wouldn't, either.

My life was so far from the King Kennedys, Dado, Kean and Djefa, Hawk—what we had been. I didn't know where I was going. But this was a step on the way. "I'll be there, Ma. Of course I will," I told her.

41

NEXT MORNING, I went upstairs and knocked on Trey's door. He leaned against the jamb, his eyes puffy from the fight, his hair in nervous twists all around his head.

"What are we doing, Trey?" I said.

He walked back into his apartment, leaving the door open. I went in after him. He sat at the edge of the ratty plaid couch. Nobody home but him.

I closed the door behind me. "Where does this end?"

"This is the life, R," he grumbled. "Take it or leave it."

"Why does it have to be this way?"

He got up and went to the window and flipped the curtain aside, looking into the street. "You punkin' out on me?"

"I'm not scared to fight, Trey. Or dance. Or whatever. I just want to know what I'm fighting *for*. At least tell me that."

He whirled around, arms hugging himself. "You wanna know what happened between me and Frankie? Motherfucker hates me 'cause I stole his girl. There, now you know."

Felt like a punch to my chest. He walked closer.

"Yeah, that's right, Ror. I stole Nessa from him three years ago, and he ain't never forgot it."

He said it like he wanted to hurt me, and it worked. I stared at his messed-up eyes, seeing their whole history—years of this battle, just over some girl.

"You're a waste, Trey Winthrop," I said. "You're really a fucking waste."

"Yeah?" He took another step toward me, threatening. "Then why you here if I'm such a waste?"

Why *was* I there? "You could be a great artist, but you're too fucking scared. You want to stay in the streets 'cause that's where the man put you. You're too scared to bust out of the mold. I guess I made a mistake about you," I said.

"Fuck that shit, white girl. You don't know nothing."

I put my hands on my hips. "Don't pull that 'white girl' shit on me. I know what I see. You got what it takes, but you ain't taking it." Was I talking to myself, too?

He stood there hugging himself, his bloodshot eyes never leaving my face.

"Fuck," I said. "Do you love her?"

He walked up to me quick, his face so close to mine I could feel his breath. "You think I ain't takin' it?" he said.

"That's right."

The moment his warm lips touched mine, I understood how cold I had been. The heat of his mouth opened up inside me, and I felt as if I was falling down, covered with sweetness, his warmth echoing in me like a drawing I used to love, a sun with rays inside rays, tripping out on ten different yellows to the solid orange center. I ran my hands over the landscape of his back, the bumps of his ribs, his skin under my palms. He held my face with both hands, then pulled off my cap, his fingers in my hair, on my torn ear, down my neck, touching me everywhere, lighting up inside me with the quiet power of a sudden flame.

He laid his warm hand over my heart and spread his fingers. He whispered in my ear, "Are you still numb?"

I would feel it now, if I stabbed myself. I would feel it if I bled.

I shook my head.

"You think I love her?"

I couldn't find words; I shook my head no.

"Ror." He took a step away. "Shit, Ror." The way he said my name scared me, like he was grasping at a tree root while falling off a cliff.

"What is it, Trey?"

He rubbed his hand over his mouth. "Nessa was there the whole time my pops was sick," he finally said.

Surprise slipped like a knife between my ribs. I didn't

want to know about Nessa, but she stood between me and him.

He punched his fist into his hand and ground it in like I wouldn't understand. "Shit."

"You feel like you owe her something?" I tried slowly.

He shook his head. "No, it's like she *owns* me," he said, "'cause she's always there. Even in my fight with fuckin' Frankie, she's gotta be there."

"Can't you just break off with her?"

"I don't wanna hurt her." He stared at his feet.

Somebody was going to get hurt. Maybe all of us.

"What about you?" I asked. "Don't *you* matter? Don't *I*?"

He looked at me as if he'd never thought of that. He touched my face like he was feeling for the true me behind it. "Nessa reminds me of my pops, that whole time he was dying. Even her smell," Trey said softly. "But you, you're so fresh, even the way you paint."

I felt my mouth opening—"Dying? Trey, you never said he *died*."

He stared at me, his nostrils flaring like he was trying to hold it in—I knew that scream—*Don't leave me.*

"We're still here," I said. "You and me."

"Yeah," he said. Then he turned away. "She'll never let me go, Ror."

Warning bells jangled inside me. "A triangle won't work, Trey. I've seen enough to know that."

He looked out the window.

I said, "Listen, let me know when you find your balls."

He choked. "What the fuck you mean?"

"You know what I mean." I ran out of his apartment before he could stop me.

42

I HAD TO SEE the old man again to get my paintings back, even though he hated me.

When I got to Jonathan's store, I went straight in, the smell of sawdust hitting me like a tired old memory. Customers wandered the aisles. His daughter sat on a stool behind the counter, her long hair streaked purple, her lips painted black. I met her eyes and swallowed hard. She knew me—she knew I'd taken the can—Nessa had told her, little birdie Nessa set up that whole damn thing to make the old man hate me. Jonathan banged something in back, and I forced myself to go up to the counter.

"Daaaaa!" she called. Heads went up; customers glanced, then looked away.

Jonathan came out, nodding when he saw me. He didn't

say anything about my bruised lip. "Didn't think I'd ever see you again."

I shook my head. "You wanted to?"

"You make it to any galleries lately?" he asked.

I thought of his lecture. Heat crawled up my neck. "Nah."

He sifted around on the counter and came up with a postcard. On the front was a black-and-white photo of a crowd; across it, in a red box, white letters said, *Don't be a jerk*.

"Go to this place," he said.

I took the card. "Why?"

"You know them watercolors you left here?"

"That's why I came back," I said.

"Well, Bettina Dillinger was here for her framing. She picked them up."

Did I know this name? "Who? What?"

"Bettina Dillinger, of the Dillinger Gallery, famous place down in SoHo?" Jon tapped the postcard. "She came in, and she liked your paintings. So, I let her take them."

"You let her take my watercolors?" I asked. My head was doing loop-the-loops.

"That's why you should go over there."

"She wanted them? What for?"

Jonathan shook his head. "Christ, I told you, Ror, you're a good artist."

I just looked at him.

He sighed. "I told her I'd send you over if you ever showed up here again. Talk to her, she'll explain it."

Even after I stole from him, Jonathan was still rooting for me. "Did you tell her what a jerk I am?"

His face softened. "I told her that you're probably about seventeen, that you probably use spray paint now, not watercolors."

I looked down, not answering.

"Am I right?" he asked.

I shrugged.

"Listen"—he unhooked a gas mask from the wall and tossed it on the counter—"you gonna keep going around painting on walls with them toxic fumes, at least use a respirator."

I picked it up, tried it on my face. "How much?"

"Get outta here," he said. "Just don't blow it with Bettina."

THEY WERE ALL sitting on the steps in front of school, too early for teachers to start harassing—Nessa and Trey, Kevin with some girl, Reuben, all waiting for the bell to ring, drawing and laughing and hanging out. I walked past Trey and went right up to Reuben and held out my hand for a slap. His jaw was black-and-blue. They were telling stories about the fight, Kevin bragging to the girl: "There's gonna be this mad dance battle in a classified spot, though I can't tell you where 'cause that info is only available to select crews. . . ."

The four of them knew where; and clearly they weren't telling me. I wondered how many more tests it would take before they trusted me with secrets.

Trey wouldn't meet my eyes. Nessa glanced at each of us, then put her arm over his shoulder, and he let her. I stepped around them and went inside.

In art class, he took his seat, but turned his baseball cap sideways to block me. I took out the card from Jonathan's, and placed it so Trey could read it. We got started cutting out our stencils with X-Acto blades. I loved the sharpness, the way the blade sliced through the paper like a knife through warm beeswax, going how I directed it, smoothly outlining each letter and tentacle.

Mr. Garci opened the ink box, and we chose our colors: one color per print, a monoprint. I picked wet plum purple. We each had a simple screen in a frame. I put my stencil on the old white T-shirt I'd brought in and put the screen on top. Squeezed ink along the top of the frame, squeegeed the ink through the screen to run it over the stencil, and then lifted the screen and stencil away.

There was my delicious violet Octora. It popped like crazy; I couldn't stop looking at it. I'd only brought in one T-shirt. I hung it to dry.

I wanted more. I got some blank paper and printed five sheets, the ink smelling like an early morning newspaper. I clipped them up next to the shirt.

I felt Sarah from the next table staring at me—no, over at my prints. She tapped my desk and said, "Hey, Ror, can I have one of those? They're really neat." I glanced at her straw-blonde hair, her dried-out lips—on her shirt, she'd printed a simple black cat.

A light went on. *Pinkie Parmigiana, the comix we used to sell.* Kids like Sarah, the especially plain kids, had the most warped hearts. They loved the strangest drawings and bought them by the armful. I smiled. "Sure, Sarah. I'll give it to you for a dollar," I said. "I'll let you have the T-shirt for five."

She thought about it for a second, then nodded and took out some money. "I'll take two prints and the shirt."

I stared at the seven dollars in my hand. My luck was changing—first the gallery and my watercolors, and now someone buying my stuff. I put the cash in my pocket, knowing exactly what I was going to do with it.

After Sarah walked away, Trey grunted. "Sellout."

"Fuck you."

"You wish."

"That's right. I do. But I ain't sharing."

He turned the bill of his cap around and looked at me with those punched-up eyes. "Meet me tonight," he said.

"Yeah? What for?"

"You wanted to go to a gallery—I'm gonna take you. But it shows real shit, not this bullshit." He pointed to the postcard.

"That 'bullshit gallery' has my watercolors."

He shook his head. "Watercolors? You don't even *do* watercolors."

"Maybe *you* don't know shit about *me*," I said.

He sent another layer of ink through his screen, hard. When he held up his T-shirt—a yellow crown—for a second, I saw into him. King of the Underground. That was all he had. I knew I wanted more than that.

After school, I went to Woolworth's and took my time selecting colors—Trey's school-bus yellow, and cosmic orange, electric blue. Then, in the abandoned building where I first saw Trey's piece, I picked a downstairs wall. I took out cosmic orange and popped the top. Shook it good, the ball bearing inside *tap-tapping* like it had a direct line to the blood in my veins. I placed the stencil in the center of the wall and sprayed onto the dingy surface in one long blast. I pulled the cardboard away—out jumped Octora. I shot another, above. Another, below. One on each side. Wild orange swimming in gray chaos. The stink of spray made my head spin; I laughed, feeling dizzy. I put on the mask and popped open yellow. Yellow was Trey. Letting my hand go free, I sprayed him over the wall, letting my heart go like it wasn't tied to anything.

I sprayed an Octora on the back of my jean jacket. I opened my sketchbook and stenciled a blue one offset slightly to the side of an orange, which made it move like a cartoon.

I could paint the world this way.

That evening, I met Trey outside, in the warm yolky light of our stoop. Inside my bag, I carried my cans and my stencil. He wore his yellow-crowned top hat with the T-shirt he'd printed. "Let's jet," he said.

We went right to the subway without talking. Being with him was like walking with a feather in my open palm.

Forcing myself not to think about being underground, on the train, I asked, "What kind of gallery is it? What's it called?"

"Yo, you'll see. Zed's got mad skills."

We changed trains twice and finally got off at a stop in the East Village. A short, dense street full of record stores, cheap jewelry sellers, fishnet-and-black-leather boutiques, Tibetan handwoven hats, incense, funny T-shirts, punked-out junkies. After that, streets of abandoned buildings—"Squats," Trey said, where kids stole electricity from Con Ed. I didn't tell him I was an expert at that. On walls and light poles, stickers overlaid glued-on flyers. Graffiti cut through all the visual noise—a ZED mural on the side of a bodega, Trey's bold ROI 85 tag on a roof ledge, a billboard overtaken by BILROCK.

I got the sense you'd never see a cop here.

We reached a park inhabited by homeless in tents and makeshift shacks. "These bros *really* got nowhere to live," Trey said. He slipped his hand into mine; I held on tight, we walked straight through. Reggae pumped from somewhere.

On the other side of the park, he let me go.

Along a wall of a black building, old glued-up flyers made me laugh out loud—Reagan's sunglasses-movie-star picture with fake headlines: RONALD REAGAN ACCUSED OF TV-STAR SEX DEATH: KILLED AND ATE LOVER.

Trey took one look and said, "Keith."

Something inside me whispered, *Like that.* This felt real.

I wanted to break out and put up what I thought, all the million different things I saw inside my head.

Underneath all the city's decay budded protest. Protest meant life. It meant struggle. It meant I should keep going until I got somewhere I wanted to be.

44

BEHIND THE GLASS storefront was a huge spray painting that said ZED 1492. Only it wasn't straight graf. From the back of a spaceship the letters shot up, then clear across the sky. A handpainted sign outside said GLAD GALLERY.

A group of guys, black, white, Rican, stood around smoking, blasting music, joking. Trading pages in their black books, markers out. Tagging every surface around them—the black-painted columns of the storefront, the metal steps, even the sidewalk itself. They ignored the two girls standing there hoping to be noticed. The girls wore white pants and slinky shirts, and turned and stared at me and Trey as we walked up. The guys side-eyed me as they slapped hands with Trey. No one held out a palm for me.

"—that was a mad piece you did on the One train, Roi. Dope."

"Yo, vandal mofo, you shoulda seen when I showed up with fifty cans of spray—"

"—hit the whole A line end to end."

Trey didn't introduce me. He made a move to go inside; I followed.

I wondered which of the guys here was Zed. On the walls hung his rectangles and squares, perfectly executed spray paintings that played with his tag.

As I looked, a bell went off in my head: canvas made the graf sellable. These pieces could hang in a museum—like Garci said, it's all about where you put something. And the prices next to them would make even Marilyn proud: three hundred, five hundred each! With that kind of money, I could move us out of our roach motel in no time.

Trey waved to the DJ by the turntables, and went over without me. Felt like he was dropping me, getting back at me, and that sandpaper started rubbing at the bottom of my stomach again.

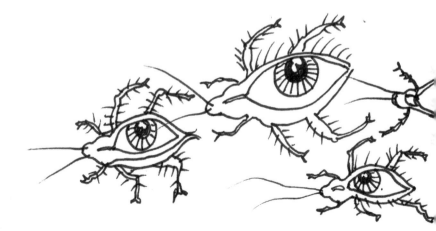

Guys pushed past me as if I wasn't there. I planted myself in front of a canvas and looked, really looked. The mix of lettering and background started a swirl of ideas—what I could do with spray. I took off my pack and lost myself in the painting until I felt a hand on my back and thought it was Trey. When I turned around, there stood a lady with cotton candy hair and a fire-engine-red smile. Glamorous from teased chignon to high heels.

"Now where did you get that jacket?" she asked. "I love it!"

"Salvation Army," I said.

She turned around. On the back of her swank black leather jacket was a cool white-line painting of a guy with a television-set head. She swung back to me with a big smile. "Keith did it for me." It was clear I was supposed to know who Keith was.

"Wow!" I said, to say something.

"One of these boys paint yours for you?"

Boys. They were everywhere, puffing on smokes and showing off their work to each other. I shook my head with disgust. "I did it myself."

Something lit up behind her eyes. "*You* did that?"

"Sure!" I started to explain my process. I was about to take out the Octora stencil when she looked to the side of me and wiggled her fingers at someone.

"Hey, I was just talking about you!" she cried.

A tall, wiry guy came over. He wore glasses painted with the same line figures he'd put on her back. I'd never seen anyone else like me who drew all over their stuff. "Trixie, baby!" he said, and threw his arms around her and walked her away without acknowledging me.

I wanted to say—*Wait a minute!*—but they were gone. He didn't see me, he wasn't interested, I wasn't worth it.

A horrible emptiness bugged me. It bugged me good. Bugged me that everyone knew each other and I didn't know anybody. Bugged me their loud talk, their laughter, their music mix blamming in my ears. Bugged me that I couldn't be seen *with* Trey.

I threw on my backpack and went out on the trashy sidewalk. Night had fallen, the streetlights settling a blue wash over the seedy bars and garbage-can stoops. On the corner, I saw a wall, virgin brown without windows, the whole side of a building, untouched by graf. I looked around at the guys— *How come no one's hit it, a pure, clean wall like that?* I wanted to ask them, but I felt too damn bugged.

I crossed the street.

I got my paints out of my backpack and lined them up. I took out my stencil—it was tiny compared to the size of the wall. Then I had the idea: I'd stencil dozens of Octoras that would shape one large one—a Reagan roach busting out lies. I thought of putting on my gas mask, but I didn't. Took a quick look around for cops and got started. Popped the tops off my cans. Down where the wall met the sidewalk, I began to spray, moving the stencil up and shaping with each color, rotating through them in a pattern, making it look like Reagan was crawling from a hole in the ground. I laughed—it moved like a Monty Python cartoon, little pieces all up the wall, legs coming from the side. My fingers were getting tired, holding the cap down, the spray coming out as fast and hard as water from a hose. All I could hear was my own breath; sweat burned my eyes. The mouth of the beetle opened over

the senile head like an umbrella, popping so hard it looked like 3-D. Bright colors on the dark background burned.

"Who the hell are you, and why the fuck you paintin' my wall?" snapped someone behind me.

I sighed and looked over my shoulder—a bunch of guys from across the street were standing there, arms folded, glaring at me. Guys, all guys; I was getting tired of their bully games. I stood up slowly. "Who's asking?"

"Who you think you are?" one of them said. His short hair stood out in spikes from his head.

I was still too bugged to be scared. "I'm from Noise Ink."

They blinked at me and looked at each other, putting things together.

"Noise Ink? You in Roi's crew?"

I nodded, even though it wasn't true, not yet.

"Since when?"

A punk in a hood said, "Wait a minute. You that girl slapped Frankie's face?"

"She slapped Frankie's face?" a dusky-rose guy asked.

"No, stupid, that was TNT did that." Some skinny kid.

I looked across the street and saw Trey and the spun-sugar woman Trixie and the TV-head guy Keith emerging from the gallery, just catching a whiff of what was going on.

Spike-hair folded his arms. "You ain't from Noise. Nobody from Noise uses them faggot stencils."

I turned to my Octora. "I do."

"Yo, Steve, get the paints," he said.

"You wanna paint with her?"

"Get the paints!"

The kid ran across the street, and Trey came over with Trixie and Keith.

"I dig that stencil," Keith said.

I glanced at him—he was serious.

"Listen, Charlie, she's down with my crew," Trey said to Spike-hair—Charlie.

I was? Did that mean I was in?

"So she said. Since when you taking on this bullshit?" asked Charlie.

Trey shoved his hands in his pockets and didn't look at me.

Keith came closer and eyeballed what I had done. "Stencil, yeah, that's good. Clean lines. You ever try wheat paste? I bet you'd make some killer posters." Why was he talking about wheat?

"Mr. Mendez will be thrilled with you going over this wall he just painted, Charlie," Trixie said.

"I didn't even do nothin' yet!"

"Come on! Mendez loves our murals," argued the skinny kid.

"Mendez will love *that*," Keith said to Trixie, pointing to my painting. "Raygun."

He got it!

She took it in, nodding. "It'll be like that painting you

have on your back. Smart," she said to me. Her look turned studious, like she was deciding on me. "Not a lot of girls painting like you."

Not a lot of girls painting, period.

Keith went on, "So you do your flyers and take them to Kinko's and make twenty copies and wheat paste them to, like, any wall. Sometimes I do a collage on a sheet of paper first, then make the copies and paste them up."

"I love your Reagan posters, Keith," Trixie said. "How come you stopped doing those?"

This was the Keith who did the Reagan poster? I looked at him closer—he was older than me. He kneeled by my paints, checking out my colors. "I just saw one of those," I said. "So, wheat paste. Is that like glue?"

He studied a label, took off a top, gave the cap a sniff. "Yeah, you make it with flour and sugar and water, just boil it up, spread it on the wall, the back of the poster, stick it on. Make sure you slap some over the poster, and voilà, it sticks real good," he said, picking up my can of blue.

That was it? That was easy. "Where did you get *your* Ray-gun idea?" I asked.

He met my eyes with a smile that said: *Where did anyone get their ideas?* "It just came." He held up the spray. "Can I?"

"Sure," I said.

He moved a little away from me and started making his comic strip TV-head guy. It wasn't graffiti, but he sprayed the same way—I watched the smooth moves of his arm, never a moment's hesitation. He didn't use words like me, just the angled drawings in blue. I picked up yellow and got back to work, wishing I could think of more to say to him.

The kid Steve came back with two milk crates of spray cans. Charlie called out colors and Steve threw them. Then he threw some to Trey.

Trey took a place on my other side and started working. Charlie got to it with his colors. Cans rattled, testing spray, getting busy. But it wasn't like being with the crew, us all working *together*. Suddenly, it felt like a contest, like the first time with Trey in Garci's class, everyone watching. Between the four of us, who would do the best painting?

We painted as high as we could reach, flipping the milk crates over and standing on them, then climbing a ladder Trixie had in the back of Glad. Wait, *she* owned the gallery?

Keith finished first—a vibrating comic strip that broke out of the borders, that made no sense unless you took time to really look, to see how all the pieces fit. I still had a can, still working while Keith slapped hands with Trey and Charlie.

Then, he patted me on the shoulder. "See you around, Octora."

Before I could answer, he took off across the street. He didn't come back.

Charlie stepped away when he was done and eyed our

pieces. Trey tossed his empty into a crate. I was the last to finish.

Four different techniques eyed us back.

Keith had his comic strip line man. Charlie was CY-BEE, done digit style, like from the future. Under it were initials—MFU, which stood for MoFo's United, his crew. I backed up to where he stood with Trey, his ROI 85 done wild style, with NI under it, *Noise Ink*. I didn't put my name or crew—the stenciled Octora was enough.

Charlie studied mine for a while, then turned to me and said, "Hey. Why don't you come on down to the 'hood? We'll hit up the bridge."

I glanced at Trey, who fingernailed paint off his thumb. I felt him waiting. "Let's all go," I said, nodding to the bunch of them.

"Let's do it." Charlie clapped his hands.

I stuffed my cans in my bag, and five or six guys stuck paints in their pockets. Charlie kicked the milk crates to the curb, and someone took back the ladder.

We walked toward the bridge, tagging walls and burned-out cars and vans as we went. I felt strange animal spirits in my blood, as if I was outside myself, felt my laughter shooting into the smog-brown night. Trey walked ahead with Charlie, some liquor in his belly, making jokes over the whine of buses. Was he scared to be seen with me? Some kids drank from paper-bag flasks, some toked up; by the time we got to the bridge, even I felt a contact high. The boys swarmed the graf-marked bridge columns that took up an entire block, the Doppler sound of cars flying overhead, loud, then disappearing in the distance.

I saw that nobody had painted higher than they could reach. The bridge was hit until about seven feet up—some scratch tags, some real nice pieces—but after that, it was blank. Forty feet up to the roadway, big and exhaust-black and blank. A forgotten part of the city perfect for painting.

I went to Charlie. "How come no one paints up there?"

He followed my eyes. "You climb up there, it's like climbing a tower. The cops can see you a mile away. Down here, it's hit and run."

"But look, it's easy climbing," I said, pointing out the scaffold-like railings that went up the column. "I'd be up and down in no time."

"Easy climb, easy bust. Everybody knows that."

"Yeah, but if you paint up there, you'll be the only name, and everyone'll see it."

"You won't know that if you a jailbird," Charlie said. I could see his shift—he was aiming to talk me out of what I was talking myself into, which made me want to do it even more.

Before he could protest, I grabbed two cans and flew up the scaffold like a squirrel. High up, the air thinned and cooled, sending a chill through me, a bubbling laugh. I could see half the city and I felt no fear, not like underground. I wrapped my legs around the metal bar at the top and reached as far as I could, clinging on with my left hand. School-bus yellow and cosmic orange against the soot-black column, where the whole goddamn world would see, I sprayed out a huge octopus screaming:

Underneath, I wrote OCTORA. I felt goddamn great. I did. Painted where nobody else dared.

I climbed back down, ready to gloat. Nobody was there. My backpack stood open on the ground, my near-empty blue untouched.

"Guys? Charlie? Trey?" I called out over the racket of traffic.

No one answered. They were gone, gone.

I felt dumb—I hadn't listened, I'd put everyone in danger and they'd flat left me. Hollow sweat broke out under my cap. I could get jumped, here alone. What if Frankie showed up? I tossed my empties into the garbagey no-man's-land under the bridge. Zipped my pack and hurried up the street.

I couldn't resist a backward glance at my painting. They might have thought I was a dope, but mine was the only name up there.

The street was too quiet. I reached the corner, almost running.

Trey stepped out from behind a column.

I cried out. Hot tears of relief blinded me for a second. I blinked them away fast.

"You know you fuckin' crazy, right?" he said.

I didn't think he was really asking.

He came close to me, his forehead dark with anger, his eyes glowing phosphorescent in the night. He put his hand behind my neck and pulled me in, and I threw my arms around him.

We kissed for a very long time.

I ALWAYS PICTURED that every time I learned a new thing, a hard wave pushed energy through my brain. Newness formed more curves: the Glad Gallery, painting the wall with the guys, Trixie and her clear-eyed smile, Keith and the wheat paste, the bridge, Trey's kisses. My head spun so much, I almost couldn't bear it. I sat in class, trying to hold steady.

I asked to be excused and went to the bathroom to clear my mind.

Nessa came in. She saw me and froze. I felt trapped, hanging on to myself, sitting on the cool radiator, pretending I wasn't there. How much did she know? Her face said: *Plenty.*

Everyone else was in class, no one around if she tried to kill me.

Fury smoke blew from her ears. She stepped farther into the bathroom, went to the mirror, and stared at herself.

"You ain't the first," she said.

I watched her back, thinking how she attacked Frankie, thinking I didn't want to tangle with her. I fingered the knife in my pocket; I was facing a girl who was as strong as me, and dangerous.

"First what?" I asked.

"First girl."

"First girl what?"

She turned cobra-like, and spit out, "*You know.* Don't make me say it." Her eyes seared guilt into me. A colorless gray drip of dumb filled my veins. Dumb cold and slimy like sewage.

I couldn't help myself. "I know what?"

She darted over and smacked the wall behind me, and I couldn't breathe.

"Shit! What, are you going to kill me?"

Her face close to mine, she said, "I should."

"But I'm not the first! You'd have to kill us all!"

I thought she was going to bite me. She pulled away.

"Why do you stay with him, if I'm not the first?" I asked.

"You don't know shit, do you, Ror?"

"What don't I know? Tell me," I said.

Another girl came in, saw us, and left.

"He's mine. That's all you need to know," Nessa said.

I folded my arms. "If you love somebody, set them free." It was the only thing I could come up with.

"Life ain't no cheesy saying."

"Maybe he doesn't want to be owned," I said.

She came close, and squinted. "Is that what he told you?"

I sighed. "He doesn't want to hurt you. Neither do I."

"You wasn't with him when his pops was dying. See if he needed me then. See if he didn't cry like a little baby in my arms." She did this really strange heave, and then burst into tears herself.

Shit. That wasn't what I was expecting.

"Aw, Nessa. Aw. I'm sorry."

She crumpled to the floor and curled into a ball. I went to her, squatted down and touched her back, then pulled my hand away. She sobbed. "I tried to be your friend, I said you could hang with the crew and this is what you do to me? Don't take him from me, don't take him away."

"Aw, shit. We didn't do anything, not really. Aw, shit. Doesn't mean anything, really, Nessa."

"We're gonna get married," she cried up into my face.

"What?" I said, looking at her tear-soaked cheeks, the makeup all screwed up.

"I had an abortion with him." She said it like they'd had a baby.

I had to stand up then. She was right. I didn't know shit about their relationship.

"Come on, Nessa"—I waved my arm around the bathroom—"You're so good at the graf." Her tags covered the walls, the unmistakable drawings of funky girls doing dance moves. "You have your whole life to go, right?"

She pressed her hands to her face, crying so hard I thought she might tear something. "He saved me from Frankie," she sobbed, "when Frankie owned my ass."

"Oh, shit." I didn't think I could hear any more. I felt my heart turning against her, I didn't know why. I just wanted to leave her, to not be near her. It was like in some sick way, she fed on these horrible things, held on to them for dear life. And Trey held on to her.

I had wanted to clear my mind; now it felt like all the curves in my brain were pulsing.

"I have to get back to class now, Nessa," I said as cold as I could.

She scowled, pushed up her sleeve, and dug her long nails

into her forearm. I saw the scars there—she'd done this before. Like the girls from the shelter.

"Damn, you need some help," I said. "I'll go get someone."

She got to her feet quick, suddenly face-to-face with me.
"You tell anyone and I *will* kill you." She went into a stall,
rolled out some paper and wiped her face. "Go back to class,"
she spat. "Go back and keep your mouth shut and leave my
boyfriend alone."

I walked out, feeling black dry coal stuck in my throat.

46

BY THE END of the day, it felt like somebody had stepped on our anthill, and all us ants went scattering—Kevin and Reuben pissed at me and Trey for going to the Glad opening without them. Nessa pissed at me and Trey for fooling around. Me pissed at Trey and Nessa for dragging me into their drama. It hurt like getting stepped on, a giant Bad Barbie footprint right on the nest of us.

All the cold shoulders made me feel like disappearing into an alternate universe.

I found a note stuffed in my locker through the vent. *We all meet at the building at midnight tonight. I'm callin a powwow. Trey.*

That night, I told Ma I was going to the corner bodega for some ice cream. She stopped her stitching, not looking up like she knew I was lying and was tired of fighting. "Just get back here in one piece. I need you for the lawyer tomorrow," she said quietly. I kissed the top of her head before I ran.

I got to the building five minutes early and heard arguing as I climbed the stairs.

". . . gone downhill since she started hangin' with us." Nessa.

"You ain't even give her a chance." Trey.

"And you ain't serious no more. She ain't no graf writer, with all that stencil shit and whatever else she's doing. Now you out painting up murals with her, like her." Reuben.

"You talkin', Rube, with all your stickers?" Trey.

"We saw it, down in the Village. She went way beyond stickers with that Octora shit." Kevin. "She's makin' you weak, Trey. She don't do it like us. She never did."

"Come on, Kev! With your nihilist writing, you gonna say that? Best thing 'bout us *is* we ain't like nobody else." Trey.

I stomped up the last of the stairs, and they shut up. I walked in the dark room lit only by flashlights up in their faces, them looking like ghouls.

"We was just talkin' 'bout you," Trey said.

"Yeah? What were you saying?"

Silence. I remembered those same mad looks from when I stole their paint. How bad I wanted to be part of them. How they gave me a chance.

Finally, Trey said: "Listen, I called y'all here tonight because we got that jam comin' up with Poison, and we need to focus. This petty arguin' shit gotta stop. We a crew, like this," he said, making a fist. "Means we stay together through thick and thin. Nobody's leavin'. We a family, that's what this shit is all about." He looked around at the sore-loser faces looking back. "Got it?"

"Why you get to break the rules?" Nessa asked.

Trey sighed, like an old man at his wife. "Yo, Nessa, I need you to kick ass on Friday, just like you know how, that's all."

"Answer her question," Reuben said. "That was fucked up, what you did, not tellin' us about the Glad opening."

I was starting to smell a mutiny, people wanting to jump ship.

Trey ignored him. "Are we gonna focus, or what?"

Kevin said, "We gotta have trust, Trey."

"Yo, look, I'm sorry, okay? That make you happy?"

"I want more than that," Nessa said.

"What do you want?" Trey's voice got tougher.

"I want you to get rid of her."

They all looked at me—I met Reuben's eyes, that betrayed look, like he'd been hoping for something between us. And Kevin, thinking I was making Trey weak. Cold fingers stabbed into my stomach.

Kevin said, "Let's take a vote."

"No," said Trey. "We need her."

"*You* need her," Nessa snarled. "*I* don't need shit."

Trey looked at Reuben. "She's good. Don't take it out on her. It's my fault." He turned to Kevin. "She don't make me weak. Ror makes me strong."

A gasp opened in me—he was admitting me in public.

"What?" Nessa's voice like ice water.

"Ror makes me strong." Trey met her eyes and held them.

"And what do *I* make you?" Nessa said.

We all waited, listening to the car alarm blaring outside.

"You drainin' me, baby."

I waited for her to kill him. Or cry.

"Now, I don't think—" Kevin started.

"Shut up!" Nessa shouted. "Let's get this out once 'n' for all. Why don't you just break up with me, Trey? Go ahead, do it!"

"I tried! You said you'd kill yourself. You think I want that?" Trey said, his voice breaking.

All the air emptied from the room.

Nessa's eyes went wild. "You think you the only male wants me?"

"No, go, fuckin' *please* go out with someone else!"

"Fine, I will!" She folded her arms. "You'll see, I will."

"Good." Trey folded his arms and snorted.

"I guess you don't need me for Friday night," she said sarcastically.

He dropped his arms, and they hung loose at his sides. His voice went limp. "No, I do. We planned this. I want you to stay with the crew, Ness. Please."

His begging bewildered me.

"We all do," Reuben said.

"Yeah, don't go." Kevin.

"I don't think so." Nessa snapped her fingers like she could make us vanish. Then she did. I heard her clattering down the stairs.

Reuben started after her, but Trey said, "No. Let her go." He took a deep breath. "That's what I always do, go after her 'cause I know she's gonna hurt herself. I stop her, yeah, but then what? It's like we stuck in the same groove."

"What about Friday night?" asked Reuben.

"Yeah, she's fierce," Kevin said.

"You keep going back to her for the same old reason," I threw in. "She's what you know. Me, I'm something different."

Kevin and Reuben looked at me—they were even more pissed.

Trey stared into his flashlight with his eyes wide open.

The boys watched Trey.

He raised his head, a decision made. "We got Ror now. Yeah, so she's different, but she's fresh. We done murals before with just one girl."

"Mural?" I echoed.

"Part of the battle is painting a mural."

Kevin and Reuben turned, expectant, like I had to prove myself all over.

I stared back. "Shit, you didn't tell me there'd be a mural, too!"

Screw them, I thought. *I'll show them. I can do it.* "Okay, well, where's it going to be?"

"Neutral turf. Down in the City Hall secret station. And that information is classified, so keep it on the down low," said Reuben.

"Underground?" I asked, feeling the familiar wave of queasiness.

"Yeah," Kevin said. "Like we been saying, it's an all-city underground extravaganza, man. Ain't you payin' attention?"

"No. I mean, yeah. Right," I said. *Shit.*

"Lotsa crews comin'," Trey said. "The MoFo's'll be there— Charlie with his boys, on our side."

"We got RTW from around the way, and TFF from Hell's Kitchen comin', too," Reuben added.

"Man, I heard they got BC from Staten Island and crews from the Bronx, and PXB from Queens," Kevin said.

It was going to be big, really big, and it was going to be underground. After what happened with Nessa, there was no way I could back out.

"What's the mural? What music we dancing to?" I asked.

Kevin took a drawing out of his pocket. The design for the mural—I saw that the four of them had been seriously planning this whole thing all along without me. Were they *ever* going to tell me? And now was I just supposed to step into Nessa's place and take over whatever part was hers—like one girl was any girl?

"What's my part?" I asked.

"You know how to paint ass?" Reuben said. Kevin laughed. What the hell?

Then I really looked at the drawing. The mural said: NOISE INK—WE KICK ASS.

"Sure," I said, feeling better. "But I do it my own way."

"You gonna use that stencil shit?" Kevin said.

"I might."

They looked at each other, then at Trey. Then back to me. "Can you even dance, Ror?" Reuben was daring me again. Kevin, too.

"You got music?"

The two of them exchanged glances with sly grins this time. "No, but we can make it."

Kevin started some beats with his mouth. Reuben sang, and I recognized his voice. It was the song they'd played in the park, after I got over the fence that first time. Were they in a band? I smiled; they were really good.

They whirled the beams around the room like lights at a concert. I let my muscles go loose, nodding my head to the rhythm. The twins said, when I used to dance with them, *Give us a fever, girl.* I let myself bounce and clap now, humming along, getting into it. I closed my eyes and pictured the bonfire, the boys keeping time, watching as I swung my hips, left, right, left, right, feeling the music in me, hot like a fever.

Give it to them. I opened my eyes. Trey watched me. I rolled my hips at him, lifting my arms up so he could see my whole body. I danced toward him. Without touching him, I circled my hands around his head, spinning and leading him into the center of the room with my fingers. Reuben sang harder and Kevin clapped to the beat. I shook my shoulders and rocked back and forth as I shimmied and boogied around Trey until he started to jam with me, his light catching the window ledge, a slash of wall. Finally, like he couldn't stand it anymore, he grabbed me close and we moved together, our thighs and knees pressing, the heat of us grinding to the tempo.

I broke free, flew like a spark in the air and landed on glass with hardly a sound.

Trey jumped after me, making freaky arc shadows along the walls with sweeps of his arms and light. We tangled and swayed. Trey dipped me. We threw our hands up, laughing while Reuben and Kevin clapped and sang like it was the Great Lawn in Central Park and they were onstage.

Finally, we stopped to wipe our sweat and catch our breath.

"I guess the girl can bust a move," Trey laughed.

"So, am I in the crew *now*?" I asked.

Reuben looked at me with warm eyes. "All's we gotta do is teach you some of our steps."

"You in," Trey said.

I let out a whoop and rubbed my hands together like I could ignite a Noise Ink flame. "Let's get busy!"

47

MA SAID TO tell our story to Lawyer Jones, that he was a good man trying to help us, to just tell him everything we could as simply and clearly as we could: how hard we all worked, what we had built. When I sat across the desk from the bald guy writing in his yellow legal pad, a map of Staten Island beside him, as he talked about strategically planning the takeover of the King Kennedys land, I couldn't help spacing out. I didn't want to conjure up dead details about the past. *I just want to think about dancing with Trey.*

"You may have to return to the property to take possession to lay a claim of rights to the land," he went on.

I'd spent the ride downtown white-knuckled on the subway. *Is there some drug I can take to get through the tunnels so I can dance and paint without puking?*

"As you know, the land is currently owned by the borough of Richmond, and it's an overlap between park land and landfill, and we may not be able to claim the whole four acres, depending on the boundaries we turn up. . . ."

We'll each have a backpack full of spray. I had spent the afternoon in the art room trying out ideas, stenciling letters onto a two-foot-wide roll of paper I found there. It was brown butcher paper, like what Dado had brought me. My letters got bigger and bigger until they became huge enough for a billboard.

I asked Mr. Garci how to mix wheat paste. He came over and looked at what I was doing and sniffed me out real quick.

"You could've gotten killed in that fight. You never know what weapons those guys carry in their pockets." He wasn't going to help me.

"I can take care of myself."

"Can you? You keep up with Trey and you'll die or just plain fade out, Ror." Garci sounded so sad and urgent, I met his eyes. I thought of that night in the tunnel, the trains at top speed an inch away from my face. *I'll have to do it again on Friday—*

"—rora?"

I shook myself. "What's that?"

"I said, tell me about this house you built with your father."

Ma and Marilyn looked at me expectantly; the lawyer's pad was full of writing.

"The dome?"

He nodded. "Yes, Aurora."

"Um, Dado and me, we built it from scrap wood we got from abandoned buildings and the landfill," I said, trying to go back in time with my words. "He always thought there was enough unused wood and nails in the world that we could live our whole lives and never have to buy anything, and we didn't. Except maybe some wire and light bulbs. Things that fray and break," I said.

Jones was writing as fast as I spoke. "Was there a foundation?" he asked. "Did you break ground?"

Dado had dug the foundation about a year before we built the dome. Everyone but Hawk had left, and it was clear that he was going soon. It was just as well. Nobody could talk to Dado by that time—nobody but me, because with Dado, you didn't use words so much as just be there by his side and see what came up.

"It wasn't that deep. Just a crawl space. We lined it with cinderblocks," I said now. "He could carry two on one arm."

The lawyer nodded. "We'll have to take a trip out to Staten Island, get some pictures. See what's left."

"There's nothing left," I said. "That's what they told us."

"If he laid cinderblocks below ground, there's something left."

I exchanged looks with Ma and Marilyn. We were running so fast away from that mess, none of us wanted to go back to see. But we had to get that money. That's what lawyers were for.

IT WAS ONE O'CLOCK in the morning, a hot June Friday into Saturday, and I was on the Brooklyn Bridge–City Hall platform with a bucket of lumpy homebrewed wheat paste. I'd made it on the hot plate when Ma wasn't there, and left before she got home. A cheap brush was in my back pocket. Under my arm was the rolled-up, spray-painted, stenciled collage, my part of the mural. In my pack, the gas mask and my share of paint.

"Come on, go, go, go!" Kevin urged behind me.

I jumped carefully down into the sewery tracks after Trey, who disappeared, yellow top hat and all.

"Under," Reuben cried from above.

I crouched and saw it there, beneath the platform: an opening big as a refrigerator tipped on its side. I took a deep breath and climbed in, trying to slow the heart that was threatening to beat out of my mouth. Putting my pack down and my poster on top, I pushed my stuff ahead of me as I crawled. The dark tunnel smelled of rat shit and rusty metal. Trey stood waiting, duffel bags slung over the shoulders of his military jacket. He helped me get out; I wished I could find a place to pee.

Reuben and Kevin emerged with their bags, and we started walking. Caged bulbs dimly lit the heavily tagged walls—we weren't the first graf writers here, not by decades. Echoes of faraway trains rumbled. I heard voices, music, wing flaps like from some kind of bats.

Trey was tense and tough. "This way," he said, heading up a few stairs into another dank tunnel. Water dripped at the far end. I shivered, despite the summer heat.

Kevin lit up a pot pipe as he walked; Reuben snapped the top of a Bud he pulled from his shopping bag. I wondered if getting drunk would rid me of this feeling—was that why people got wasted?

A few more turns, and now I didn't know the way back.

"Up here." Trey scaled a thin metal ladder. I followed up after him, and down another tunnel. Down some stairs, into a hole. I could see, at the end, a big space filled with light.

We came out into an enormous, ancient platform that had long ago been abandoned. I stood stunned for a moment, staring at the high arched walls, the intricate mosaics of dusty

Art Deco patterns made back when people cared how stuff was designed. You could still see how gorgeous this place had been.

Voices shouted from far down; a Chaka Khan song wailed hot and grindy. Behind a wall at the opposite end was another space made of ugly, tagged concrete blocks, a perfect forgotten zone. There, a horde of bodies gathered, and guys and girls in their summer best were coming from above, down metal ladders from grates like the ones in the street.

"Must be like a hundred bros piling in," Kevin breathed.

"Shit, why didn't we come in *that* way?" I asked.

"Cops see you comin' in that way." Trey moved his hand nervously over his mouth. "Why they all crowdin' up like that?"

Kevin said, "Don't those skanks know the number one rule? Don't draw attention to yourself. Be stealthy and slick."

"Toys and hos, all a them." Reuben's deep voice ricocheted against the walls.

Trey muttered under his breath, "No class," and waved us on. We put our stuff away by a whitewashed stretch; Trey slapped palms with the two guys who would guard it.

My stomach pinched: over there, Frankie in the middle of his boys, all of them in Kangol hats. The sight of him made me wish again I was home in bed. Behind them, girls piled in, dressed for clubbing in black lace and teased hair and fishnet stockings. When they hit the ground, they joined the dancers. The air was thick with weed and cigarette smoke. Against the far wall, a Rasta guy in a saggy blue hat stood near three boom boxes and a couple of turntables, watching the writhing bodies like a scientist ready to add another needed chemical.

"DJ Capgun," Trey told me.

"Tell me again, how do we know when to jump in?" I asked.

"Cap'll start it. Between each dancer, there's a vote. When it's your turn, I'ma tag you. Then you do that thang we practiced, R." He reached for my hand and gave it a squeeze. I didn't want to let him go.

When Capgun saw us, he lowered the music. A complaint went up, then everybody turned and realized why. Charlie and his guys and some of the crews moved to our side. A space cleared in the center, and I imagined myself an eagle soaring so high above this mob, they'd seem too small to worry about.

Capgun said, "Yo, yo, yo, make room for Poison Crew goin' up against the mad Noise Ink in a psycho cypher. Noise'll school ya, Poison'll fool ya, put your hands together for the crews that'll rule ya." Kids pushed their bodies up into us so they could see. Capgun put on "The Message." The synthesizer bounced against the walls, and Grandmaster Flash's words started.

Trey stepped out. Across from him, Frankie strutted into the circle wearing parachute pants and Pumas. It stopped Trey cold for a second. When they were filling me in on who would dance against who, the boys said Frankie never danced, yet here he was, gyrating his hips, all his muscles rippling, the kids going wild, shouting, "Look at Frankie get down!" Even I couldn't take my eyes off him.

Trey stuttered into his robot moves, and I screamed for him, along with everyone on our side, "Trey's rockin' it!" I could feel Kevin and Reuben pushing into me, telling me to get ready. They guessed I'd go opposite a guy named Nick. My limbs whizzled with nerves. I ran my eyes over the boys across from me, ready to run Nick over with my moves.

Trey was picking up speed now, throwing the kicks, dancing in circles around Frankie. Frankie swayed and popped like a useless elephant. Capgun mixed in a new song, a faster rhythm, a smashing cymbal and a screaming girl. Trey finished with a moonwalk, and everyone went wild as he turned and smacked my hand. Boos chased Frankie off the floor. His ranks opened up to let through his dancer just as I jumped to the center.

Damn. That wasn't Nick. It was Nessa.

I stumbled away from her, trying to keep my body moving to the clashing song. She came after me, to catch me in her white Adidas. I let myself feel the music, the beat racing through my blood, heating me all over. I got mad, as pissed as Dado on a night in the forest thinking the spooks were after him. I flipped and flared straight for her like hunting a traitor. I met the hate in her eyes with the force of my own. She sideswiped me, pulling away at the last second, then shook her chest at me with that harem-girl bullshit, sending a frenzied howl up from the boys. I jumped three times at her, folding my arms and kicking like a Communist. Then I Backed the Bus Up like Trey showed me until I hit bodies. They pushed me back in.

She and I sprang into the center of the ring at the same time, our faces nearly touching.

If we were on fire, we would've burned each other.

The first notes of another beat started. Nessa skipped to the edge of the circle to cheers like fucking Rocky. When I threw my arms out, boos deafened my ears. I saw Kevin reaching for me. A touch-tone phone dialed inside the music, then ringing, then a guy saying, "Yo, B, answer the phone . . ."

Kevin yanked me out, and I made my way through the herd to catch my breath and wipe my sweat. They thrust me toward my crew. I pushed back my cap and tried to slow myself, my brain flying, feeling Nessa huffing and staring across from me. Clapping made her the winner between us, but to me she was still a loser. What kind of girl would swap crews like that? Especially if it was true, what she claimed about Trey saving her from Frankie. That dumb thug was putting his arm around her, like she was his property—and Trey was glaring at them like a mad dog. Mrs. Hyde percolated in my blood, the green ooze that made me want to rip Nessa's eyes out.

Fuck, I didn't want to be like that.

Trey elbowed over to Poison's side. I met Nessa's eyes, a shit-eating grin across her face that said *See, Trey still loves me.*

Kids screamed, "Yo, Nil be smokin'!" Still, loud applause from the throng said the other guy won. Kevin switched off with Reuben to some rap, and a short kid spun in like a top. Everybody hollered their lungs out.

Trey went up to Frankie and jammed into him. Rage blinded me. What was all this for, if we were going to fight for real?

I fisted my way around the circle just as Frankie was muscling Trey back. Grabbed Trey's arm and glared at him and shook my head. It was like something went out of his eyes when he saw me. He stepped away from Frankie, who had raised his hands, ready to fight. Trey came back with me to our side.

And then, that was it—we had no more dancers left for the cypher. The crowd cheered and booed.

Capgun declared Poison the winner, and I wanted to crush him, to argue until he changed his mind, till they all did, those faces mocking us. He put on another song, and everyone boogied like nothing had happened, filling up the empty space in the middle.

I stood next to Trey, not wanting to touch him. He did that in front of them all—went over to Poison's side to fight. Everyone saw he still loved Nessa. I had come down here for him, for our crew, and now I just wanted to go, to leave, to not be involved with this beautiful boy who would tear my heart out and make me eat it.

But I had a mural to put up.

49

FRANKIE AND HIS boys moved over to their half of the white-washed wall and started pulling out spray cans from old gym bags. One of them unfolded a ladder, and I saw Reuben come from behind the tagged concrete block carrying another one for us.

We took our places.

I was at the edge of our side—in the middle of the wall, next to Nessa. She cut her eyes at me.

Heckling rippled through the crowd—*Cat fight! Toy girls!*—and I wished I had earplugs.

The crews fanned out on either side of us. On my right, Trey and the boys set out our colors. Since my word was the last one in the mural, I would stay on the ground while the guys worked the ladder around and above me. Smoke and voices and music congested the air; if I had blinders, I'd be able to focus. I thought of putting on my gas mask, but nobody else had one.

Enough. I had to get busy.

I picked up a can of neon red. Neon, like freon, like cold chlorofluorocarbon right through your bones. In a few long sweeps of my arm, I had the outline of Octora. Nessa did her TNT. I stepped back for some breaths, then came in again. Working in purple and green neons, I filled my foundation. I was getting better at this. Faster. A lot faster.

With my name done, I opened my bucket of glue and slapped it along the wall and under the ladder with the brush in thick white lines, trying to chase out the lumps. No matter who won the dance, we would win for our goddamn mural; I was sure about that.

It was time to reveal my brown paper masterpiece. I took off the rubber band and unrolled it onto the ground. Intense saturation of colors and layers and flavors. People scrunched in behind me to see.

"Ho, snap! Look what she done!" Some kid in a tracksuit.

"Dang, Frankie's gonna shit when he sees that!"

I could feel Nessa and their boys looking.

Quickly, I flipped it and brushed on a thin layer of paste. I picked it up, and, using the brush, started smoothing the painting out over the length of the wall.

"Yo, Octora, you be buggin'!" Steve and Charlie jumped

in to help me flatten it down. As I cleared off the glue, more
and more people gathered, their voices rising above the din.

"That's cold, girl."

"Fresh!"

"Def! Check it out."

Behind me, firecrackers went *pop-pop-pop*, and I thought
they were getting a little carried away.

"It's the cops! Man, it's the cops, everyone split!"

The cops? I heard a crazed scramble and a swell of shouts,
and turned around. The cops? I tried to think. To move. People

raced by. *The pigs are here? How do I get out?* The music cut off, kids screamed, some shoved against me. The ladder fell with a crash, nearly knocking me over. I stood perfectly still as if I could become invisible.

The cops, *the pigs*—we never had a run-in on Staten Island. It was one of the first things Dado had taught us kids. We were all so careful. I never got caught. Inside me screamed *Run!* but my legs wouldn't move. Fear leaned into my chest like an anvil.

The madness of the crowd froze me.

If Trey hadn't—

If I hadn't followed him down—

What am I doing?

Everyone stampeded the ladders up to the grates, but flashlights shone down, stopping them, so they reversed, went other ways, psychotic with terror like roaches in the sudden light.

I watched, my whole world gone berserk.

I didn't belong here, this wasn't my scene—this wasn't me. With Dado, this wouldn't have happened. None of this would've happened. We wouldn't be doing this at all.

Reuben was no longer beside me. Neither was Kevin. Or Trey. I heard the *thonk thonk* of hard rubber shoes on metal ladders, and saw the men in blue. Kids disappeared like rats down holes while the men scurried after them. One yanked a guy's jacket over his head, slamming him to the ground.

A man in a blue NYPD sweatshirt snagged my arm and

twisted me toward the wall, shouting that I was under arrest. The moment he touched me, the whole thing shattered apart like broken glass—this world, graffiti.

My life was over. I fought him like a dog, trying to get loose.

He snatched a can from the ground and sprayed it in my face, blinding me. I screamed, pain blazed into my head, a blackness I couldn't blink through. I tried to run, to free myself as I howled and clawed the paint from my eyes—

My eyes, shit, my eyes, I need my eyes—

I heard him grunting, "Stop moving, you bitch," as he tried to keep hold of me.

I heard a *clunk*, like someone hit the guy with a bagful of cans, then felt other hands on me, pushing at me, and a scared voice telling me to shut up and keep moving. I let myself be dragged forward, still blinded. I promised myself if I got out of this tunnel alive, I would never paint underground again. I would never take another train anywhere.

"Fuck," I heard him muttering, "fuck, fuck, I *knew* it. I *knew* this was gonna happen."

Trey. He came back for me. This was all his fault.

As he pulled me, I rubbed at my eyes, trying to clear the spray paint. I felt it burning into me, clotted on my lashes. Tears bucked out of my lids. Everything was a blur.

I wasn't built for this shit.

We were in the back tunnels then, deep in the underground station maze. Trey led me through the cold space, down the ladder, over the hole, murmuring where to go the whole time.

We crawled to the end of the platform tunnel and sat there catching our breath. I'd left everything behind—my paste, my brush, my backpack, my stencils—it didn't matter. I had nothing, and it didn't matter. I didn't care. I didn't want it anymore.

"I can't see!" I moaned. I shook. My whole body was wet with tears and sweat and fear.

I heard him moving around. Then I felt him rubbing some kind of cloth over my eyes; I smelled the coconut of him.

I was crying, sobbing, "What happened? I don't even know what happened."

"Shh, now. They'll hear us." He worked at my eyes, clearing them.

I stuttered in my cries and blinked and blinked, my vision coming back as he wiped at the paint.

"I—I think I'm starting to see." I began to make out his face, his caramel eyes clearly worried. His T-shirt was off. When he saw me able to look at him, he tied the shirt over my head like a bandana.

He crammed his arms into his jacket. Somewhere along the line, he'd lost his top hat crown. He looked pitiful without it. Not so royal.

"We gotta make a move," he said. "We can't stay here."

He scootched to the opening, and from his inside pocket took out a mirror attached to a car antenna that he stretched to its full length. Stuck the contraption out onto the tracks and used it to look up and down and onto the platform. "All right, this is simple," he told me. "You just get out onto the tracks and follow me inna that tunnel. We're gonna walk to the next station, away from the Five-O crawlin' all over here, jump onto the platform, and get on a train home like you ain't got a faceful of paint. Got it?" he said.

My eyes still burned. Everything was wavery. "I can't."

"Let's go." He stepped out and reached in and seized my arms and dragged me out of that tunnel.

50

WE GOT OUT at our stop and ran up the stairs to the street. Trey zipped into a bodega for a jar of mayonnaise, and we went up to the sixth-floor bathroom and barred the door shut. He filled the sink with warm water and sat me on the floor with the mayo.

I couldn't help crying salty tears that stung my smarting eyes, the world a fog in front of me. "I can't . . . I don't know how I got into this," I wailed.

"Hush up." He took his T-shirt off my head and threw it into the water. Then he opened the jar, scooped up the cold mayo, and smeared it onto my forehead, up into my hair. My skin revolted at the cold. I felt glad I could see him; I didn't want to look at him.

"I'm a dope," I cried.

"Shut your eyes," he said.

"I'm a total fucking loser. I can't do this. I can't."

"Cut the pity shit or I'ma put some ham on you and eat you," he said. I felt his cigarette breath on me, his fingers working the oily glop into my eyelids, gently down my lashes. The mayo smelled of egg. His expert hands rubbed at my cheeks, soothing me. I sniffed, my sobs dying down. "You scared of the cops," he said then.

I wouldn't admit it to him.

"You scared of the tunnels, you scared of bein' underground, you scared of the subway, you scared of the Five-O—"

"All right, already!"

"What the fuck you wanna be a graf writer for, then?" he asked, like he was really curious.

I couldn't answer that.

"One thing for sure," he went on, "you ain't scared of high places. I seen you on that bridge like a fuckin' chimp."

I breathed in, breathed out. Heard the water drip. "Maybe I ain't a graf writer," I finally said.

"You a graf writer and you an artist. You a graf artist. You could suck and be a toy, but you don't suck. You just scared shit. That's your weak spot. Work on it."

I heard him squeeze the water out of the T-shirt. He pressed its heat into my eyes, as if trying to melt the pain.

"Once you're king of the lines," I asked him, "then what?"

He sighed. "My daddy called me poppy show. He said I got

to be ginny gog. That's irie, fadda." He squeezed out the cloth again, and washed me.

"What's that mean?"

"He said graffiti was a lot of chobble—trouble. I'm a show-off. I should be a politician." He shook his head. "He never got past bein' a fuckin' bus driver."

"You talk to your dad in your head?" I asked.

He didn't answer as he wiped my lids again. "Open," he said. When I did, I could tell the paint was washed clean from my lashes. I looked at his smart Stokely Carmichael eyes and knew he had some plan for himself, one he couldn't explain to me.

His plan wasn't my plan. Neither was Garci's, or Jonathan's. I'd have to make my own. I needed some rules—my own fucking manifesto. Right now, going along with the crew, I was shutting off who I had been with Dado. The things he taught me. Right now, I was ruled by the law of unintended consequences.

That was no way to live.

Trey scooped up a handful of mayonnaise and wiped it on my mouth, and then, with his thumb, rubbed it around and around, getting my pulse going. If only he wasn't so damn fine.

I held his arm still. "You keep doing that and I'm going to put cheese on you and eat you," I joked nervously.

"Stop talking." He took the wet cloth and rubbed the

mayo off my mouth. Then, he came close and licked my lips. "Mmm, creamy."

"Do it again," I said.

He sat on the tile in front of me and pulled me close. "I love when a girl's all slick," he said, running his fingers through my mayonnaisey hair.

"Any old girl?"

"You."

He put his mouth on mine and I fell into his hot cocoa world. Something inside me didn't want it. Didn't want to hurt like this. Didn't want to follow him so hard and fast that I forgot to hear my own fear. Dado always said it, *Stay quiet, listen to the warnings inside.*

With Trey, in Noise Ink, I couldn't stay quiet enough inside.

I pulled away and said, "Would you hate me if I quit the crew?" *They left the King Kennedys one by one, to save themselves.*

His pupils were big, swallowing his eyes. He swiped his mouth with the back of his hand. "You scared of me, too?"

"I'm scared of the pigs."

"We hit playgrounds, ball courts, construction sites. Ain't no pigs there." I heard the tightness in his voice, impatient with my fear, yet wanting to convince me.

"I don't know, Trey."

"We go to the East Village, hit the walls like Charlie, like Keith. Our crew backs you up when you do shit. Ain't nothin' to be scared of."

I thought of the way he bopped that pig and dragged me away. I never wanted to feel that terror again. I dropped my head. When I didn't say anything, Trey got up and threw down the wet T-shirt as if he was done with me, getting ready to leave me with my hair full of paint and mayonnaise.

I scrambled to my feet, stood beside him, and looked in the mirror—like damn Halloween looking back. My eyes two irritated circles, paint turning my skin tomato red, my hair drooping with the weight of wet, smelly glop. My cap long gone. Next to me, Trey looked sexy as hell. I just looked like hell.

"I showed you how to use spray, R. I gave you that idea for the fuckin' octopus. I brought you to Glad Gallery. I took you into the crew when none of them wanted you."

"It's just—I'm not sure I'm cut out—"

He put his hand up like he didn't want to hear any more. "Fuck it, Ror. I knew you was a soft yellow banana." He turned and threw open the bolt and slammed his way out of the bathroom.

51

THAT SATURDAY TURNED out hotter and more humid than any had been so far. June heat fermented the exhaustion in my bones into a weird popping energy, and I just couldn't stay asleep. Eyes closed, I listened to my sister dress for work, a perfect girl on her perfect way to the ice-cream shop. I picked at my hair with furtive fingers. A warm shower and a nub of soap had gotten off all the mayo, but still I could feel the hard paint in my bangs and deep in my nostrils.

Mid-morning, Ma got up and folded the sheets from the couch and turned on the TV. The sun hid behind heavy rain-clouds. Thunder rumbled and cracked. Rainy wind brought me out of bed. I shut the window as water threw itself in streaks down the glass. While she hand-sewed tank dresses on the couch—ones she'd designed with Marilyn, perfect for

this sweltery summer—Ma watched the news. I eased myself
beside her.

"I'm not going to ask you why you came in at dawn this
morning," she said without looking at me.

Yellow.

"I'm not going anywhere today," I said.

"I'm not going to ask you about that paint on your face
and in your hair."

I ran my hand over my bangs.

"I'm just going to tell you that I fear for you, but I love you
no matter what, Ror."

I pressed my cool fingertips into my hot eyes. I just
wanted to be there with Ma, listening, feeling, breathing,
being. News came on about the fallout from the Olympics.
After that, a story about a police officer shot with his own
gun. Police officers; I never wanted to see another one. He
was just doing his job, the news said, stopping a man from
stealing a pair of glasses when the thief stole his gun and
shot him.

Just doing his job.

Was that cop just doing his job when he shot me?

Was that even *legal*?

I wanted to get it down, what happened. I started for my sketchpad, then remembered I had lost everything. *Got to stop doing that.* I dug around for an old school notebook, and used that instead.

Through the floor came downstairs neighbors yelling out curses in Spanish; from the halls, kids screeched as they chased each other up and down the stairs; outside, an angry rain tried to clean the dirty city streets.

A commercial came on—Reagan's reelection campaign ad. The words made me look up from my drawing.

"It's morning again in America. . . ." a voice said.

I wondered what America Reagan lived in. Not my America. Not the street I lived on, not the projects one neighborhood over, not the kids with sick parents or no parents at all. Forget it if you were seventeen and needed help. Would Reagan turn into an octopus if he told the truth in his ads?—"Okay, folks, I'm going to give all the money to big businesses so they can kick back some to me. I really don't care about the rest of you. Fuck off and die. Just make sure my friends at General Electric keep their corporate jets. Our America's run on crisp dollar bills and fat accountants."

Those tentacles.

Yellow.

This was a country where the only place for an artist like Trey was the street. Where a girl had to become one of the

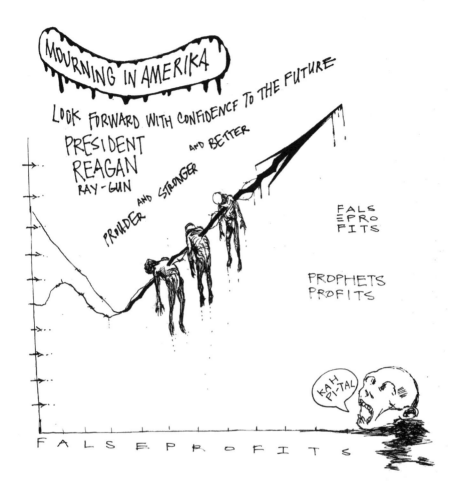

boys or to give herself over to some guy just to be taken seriously.

I didn't want to end up like that. Dead or lost or just plain
faded away.

I FELT THE CALL of grass and trees, the cry of dirt. Early Sunday morning, before anyone else was awake, I walked through the rain-washed streets to Central Park feeling as alone as a person could ever feel. I entered the park without seeing anyone else.

Breathing in the tree-fresh, grass-bright air damp as morning dew, the past months, weeks, days went by in my mind like pictures. The fire. The shelter. Finding spray paint. Running after Trey and the crew. Painting underground. Fighting with Frankie. Octora. Meeting Trixie. Watching Keith paint. The bridge and the cypher. Getting hit by the cop.

When I sat on a bench and took out my notebook, a question came at me hard and fast: Why couldn't I decide for *myself* what and where I wanted to paint?

Octara's Manifesto Destiny
my
Emancipation ~~Proclamation~~
from the slavery of Brain washing
for the good of all -kind-

WON: always make something that opens a gasp inside the second TURN of your large intestine.

TOO: do it in a place where you can take your time, where no one hunts you like a mouse under the radiator, or a fucking elephant in AFRICA

FREE: Yes, stay free of entrapments, tricks, sick love, expectations, set-ups, fall downs, unreal dreams and unintended consequences, feel FREE to fuck up.

FOR: ever, lasting, true, deep.

FIFE: with play music you can dance to, make sure you dance with people who can see your moves, get out before the music stops and the party ends, and the cops come to shut you down.

SEX: Do I want that, or do I want love?

S-HEAVEN: Keep Dado up there where he belongs. "I'll meet you in the next WORLD."

ATE: McDonald's is your kind of place, hamburgers in your face, french fries up your nose, pickles between your toes — I want my money back before I get a HEART ATTACK.

I would follow my own manifesto; my own rules. Not Dado's, or Tristan Tzara's, or the constitution of the United Untied States. Not Noise Ink's. This one would have laws I could break and still stay free.

I looked up to see a squirrel watching me. I remembered a day back at the end of the King Kennedys: No one else was there. Even our animals were gone. I sat just like now with a notebook, talking to myself, when a squirrel came over and shook its bushy tail, staring at me. I had talked to it aloud, I was so lonely, until even it scurried away.

I didn't know what it would be like to go back to school, to face everyone again. The boys had left me. What Trey had said wasn't true—they didn't back me up. When it came down to it, it seemed like all anyone cared about was themselves.

THE SIDEWALK WAS choked with more than the usual suspects. As I walked up to school with Marilyn, I expected, as always, that appreciative eyes would admire her outfit of the day, acting as if I wasn't there until I drifted off. But people came up and started talking, yapping over each other in some kind of mumbo jumbo, all of them looking at me.

"Frankie's an ass, yo!"

"Is it true *you're* Octora?"

"And you hit that wall with Keith downtown!"

"And the AURA piece on the train! It's yours!"

"What about the one on the bridge? You see that shit!"

"See it! Man, I was *there!*"

They touched me, pulling me by the shoulders to face them. I shook my head. *How did they know? What did they want me to say?*

Over their voices, Marilyn turned to me, eyes worried. "Rora, what's going on?"

Kevin came over, put his skateboard up as if to block me from them, told them to back off. "Take a chill pill now, y'all, just chill." I didn't want to show Kev how glad I was to see he had escaped the cops. And how angry I was that they'd left me.

Marilyn said, "Hey, kid, I'm her sister, what's going on?"

This was *my* deal. "Marilyn," I said. "I got this." She met my eyes over the crowd with curiosity, maybe even a little awe. I saw her stare as Kevin pushed me toward the door.

He handed me something.

It was my backpack. I zipped it open quickly; my pads, stencil, pens, even a can of spray was still inside. The paint opened up a rush in me; I missed the weight in my hand, the way it went on the wall. I missed it like a person. I closed the bag and clutched it to me.

When we got inside, I asked him, "What's this all about?"

"After the blue boys split, me and Reuben went on a recon mission and picked up all our paints and shit. Weren't gonna let those fuckers win."

We back you up. Trey came for me. He saved me. And the boys went back for our stuff.

Kevin went on, all lit up. "Ror, man, you hear what happened to Frankie?"

I shook my head. "No, what?"

"He got busted! They sent him to Rikers yesterday. Now

everybody's freaking out. Saying he got his face slapped by *another* girl. First it was Nessa in front of school, then—you."

"Me?"

"That ASS you painted with Frankie's name, man, *everybody* seen it. That's what all those fiends outside are talkin' 'bout."

"Wow. Shit. I thought, when the cops came—"

He clapped his hands. "Man, I took off," he said. I could see he hadn't thought anything about leaving me that night.

"Where'd you guys go?"

"We ran down the tunnel and hid till they left. Yesterday, Trey told us about you, said you got sprayed in the face." He wiped my forehead with one finger, like I still had some there. "You okay?" he asked softly.

"Yeah, I guess." So Trey hadn't said I wanted to quit the crew.

The bell rang, and we went to class.

After, I walked through the halls, aware of eyes *staring* at me. For the first time in that school, I felt *seen* by those strangers, like I'd been hiding and somebody had pulled away my mask, and there I was. Revealed.

Before English, Reuben came up and traded handshakes with me. He even gave me a hug. He said it was all over the city, what I did. "But the Five-O took Frankie away, so you lucky he ain't comin' after you, Ror. Otherwise, we'd have to put you into the witness fuckin' protection program." He laughed.

Just then, Nessa came around the corner, running into us, then stopping short and staring. She blew out a laugh at me. "You one pitiful bitch," she said.

"Least my boyfriend ain't in jail," I shot back.

Her fists came up, and Reuben stepped between us.

Nessa put her open hand in Reuben's face, then walked around him, away. She didn't look back.

"I don't think she'll bother you, Ror," he said, watching her go. "Everybody knows what went down. That you beat her at the cypher. That she went back to Frankie. She just feels stupid she's on the losing team."

"I didn't think I beat her."

"That's the word on the street."

We went into class, and he actually sat next to me.

Kids looked at me all day. Sarah with the straw hair was wearing my Octora T-shirt. I gave her a thumbs-up when I passed her in the hall. She came over with two girls trailing behind her.

"Hey, Ror," she said like we knew each other real well. "My friends here want to know if they can get a shirt off you."

One of the girls had square metal glasses, the other a spray of freckles. I shrugged. "Um, yeah—sure, five bucks each. I can make them for you tomorrow, I guess."

The girls handed me the money and the three gave each other a giggle like I was some kind of famous person, and they walked away.

Another girl came up, a nervous-looking brown girl with straight black hair. "'Scuse me, you're Octora, right?"

I glanced around. "Who wants to know?"

"You the one beat Frankie, right?" she said.

"That's what I heard."

"Can I get one of those T-shirts from you?" the girl asked.

"For five bucks you can."

She handed me the money, and I said she'd get it when I had art class. Art class. The only person I hadn't seen all day, I realized, was Trey.

I WAITED FOR Trey before going into art. When he didn't show up, I went to Mr. Garci and asked if I could screen-print the old T-shirts I brought in.

"Ror, you need to start taking yourself seriously."

Jonathan said the same thing. *You need to work seriously.*

"I work hard!"

"Is that right? When you draw, do you think about who's going to see it? Is it something we can put in a portfolio for college?"

A portfolio for college? I sighed. More school? Like Marilyn? It hadn't done much for Dado, for anyone at the King Kennedys. I wanted to break out. Bust the mold.

"I'll make you a deal, Ror," Garci said. "You promise me you'll work on a portfolio—actually work—and I'll let you print those shirts."

Then I remembered the Dillinger Gallery. Bettina Dillinger. Like Trixie. How many women ran galleries? How many women were in them? "I think I have a few pieces already, Mr. Garci. These watercolors I did." I'd have to get them back. If I wanted to be serious, I'd have to go there and face her, find out why she took them in the first place.

He grinned big. "That's the spirit! The ink is in the box."

At the end of the period, when I came out of the classroom, Trey was standing there. He handed me a photograph and walked away. I took one look—it was the first octopus I'd painted underground, the AURA, me with a lopsided smile on my face.

"Hey, wait up!" I ran and called after him just as he pushed the door open and went out of the building, into the blinding sun. "Wait, dammit!"

Outside, he leaned against the dirty white brick, stringy tags swirling up the wall behind him, arms folded, that cool stare under the brim of his baseball cap.

Kids sat fanning themselves with comic books, throwing bologna at each other, watching us out of the edges of their eyes.

"I'm not yellow," I said to Trey.

He pushed himself off the wall and started walking away.

I followed. "I mean, I just, you know, I don't like the idea of getting killed."

At the corner, he turned real quick and said, "You throwin' away a perfect opportunity."

"What do you mean?"

"Since the cypher, your name's got around. Now you can build on your fame. On *our* fame, Noise Ink *crew*."

"Oh." I saw how he saw it. What Garci said about Warhol, about *using* the attention on you, not letting *it* use *you*. Or not letting anyone else use you. "I mean, I'm still with the crew. But like, I also, I want to go off on my own sometimes, too." I was trying hard not to hurt him. "I mean, when I'm not doing something with the crew in a park or somewhere in the city where we—where we won't get—where the cops won't see us. I'd like to, you know, try things out."

He nodded slowly. Like he saw right through me but I should keep talking.

"I mean," I went on, "of course I'm with Noise Ink, right? I'm family. I'm in the crew."

His brows relaxed a little.

"Just—I want to paint where I can take my time. I need to figure some stuff out on my own, man," I said. The words stuttered and trickled out of me, like an almost-empty can. "I mean, yeah, I'm scared of the cops. I don't know if I can paint where I might get caught without being scared. But that may take me some time to—to feel out where I'm not scared. Give me some time?"

"What kind of time?"

"I don't know."

We stood there together on the corner, people pushing past us, traffic going by as the light changed and we didn't cross.

I went on. "Trey? Just—don't cut me off. Let me figure it out."

He kicked at the lamppost.

Finally, he held out his hand. I gave him a slap, and he hung on to my fingers. "Aight. I dig," he said.

We walked together to McDonald's. On the way, I told

him about the T-shirts and the money, and when we got there,
I bought him a burger.

"Maybe I'll go with you sometime," he said. "To where
you're not scared."

We looked at each other for a moment.

Then we shared a sack of fries.

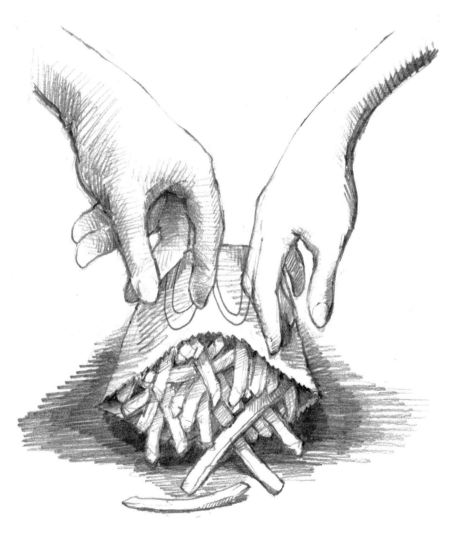

MY RIDE DOWN to SoHo on the M5 bus took twice as long as the number 1 train—plus an extra hike from the bus stop—but it was worth it to avoid going underground. I'd discovered buses were better for sketching, anyway. I sat in the back, the window open wide, my feet up on the ledge, drawing a mother with cornrows sitting across from me. She was trying to read a book, and her daughter kept pulling at her hair, her ears; occasionally, like a lioness, she would bat her cub away, and the kid just wanted some love. They got off near Penn Station, and an old couple threw their tokens in and sat down, the two of them like a set of dolls you could neatly fit into each other, they had become so similar.

I got off at Broadway and Houston and found my way going west on a wide street with cars traveling both ways. I didn't know what I was expecting when I thought of SoHo,

but it wasn't traffic like an expressway. I cut off the main block to a narrow cobblestone street. Buildings hunched together squat and giant, architecture old and ornate like from the last century. I felt myself looking up at the columns and scrolls and fancy arches that made up the construction and wondering how they built it.

Here, there were no tags, no pieces like across town, but on a creamy outside wall, someone had plastered an abstract figure painting and signed it AVANT. I stopped. I resisted the urge to take out a marker and add an S to make it SAVANT. I stuck my fingernail under it, but it was thick cardboard glued down good. I ran my finger over the paint—a latex, or acrylic. I looked around at a clump of girls in skin-tight dresses and red lipstick, a woman in a peach power suit hurrying behind them, two couples in bleach-splattered jeans talking too loud. Inside me, a smile opened up like sun-ray fingers reaching to the sky.

I wanted to see more. I walked ahead.

In a corner parking lot, posters announced Bands! Clubs! Nights of Music and Drawing! I took out my pad and wrote the addresses down. On the next block, on a gray building, someone had stenciled a white angel with a long devil's tail. Down another side street, a life-sized painting of a man in silhouette dripped down a wall, an arrow shot through his head. Above, it said: NO NUKES, THIS IS YOU. I laughed and walked on.

Hidden between two brick buildings, I spied painted fingers taping over a painted crack in a painted brick wall. I stepped out of the human traffic to look, inside me the lightness opening into disbelief. I had that feeling like at Glad Gallery watching Keith paint, like he got it, got me, and I wanted to know more where his ideas came from. Glad. I hadn't gone back; did I belong there?

In this place, I felt like I didn't have to ask that question. In this place, I saw it all around, in a whisper, in a notion, in a phrase. In an image.

This was where I wanted to be.

When I got to West Broadway, the street widened with glass storefront galleries. The first had an enormous black-and-white photo of a kitchen sink in the window. Something about it drew me inside. The smell hit me—these were not photos but oil paintings. I had tried oils, a gooey medium that took forever to dry, that demanded layers and patience I definitely didn't have. This artist did. People in black jeans and T-shirts drifted past as I studied the flat surface of each painting. I could not figure out how the artist made it look so shiny.

Back on the street, I wove in and out of other galleries to look at paintings and photos and sculptures, collecting postcards, feeling the beams of light that made the smile open in me. I sketched ideas and revelations, hearing Dado's voice singing Blake—

Walking among the fires of hell, delighted with the enjoyments of Genius; which to Angels look like torment and insanity

He must've felt destroyed by the galleries that dismissed him. How would they see me?

I found myself standing in front of the Dillinger Gallery. The name was elegantly gold-painted right onto the dark brown exterior. You couldn't see inside, like they were protecting some great secret. A long-haired man in leather pants and a pirate shirt burst from the door, a girl in a catsuit behind him. They laughed as they passed me. She held the door open until I went in.

The show I was expecting, the artist Kruger with her red-and-white *Don't be a jerk* pasted across crowds, was no longer there. Instead there hung abstract paintings big as me, wide as my arms outstretched, colors quivering straight across the room like a mambo. Lemon streaks tried to sneak out from under the weight of a red, blues oozed into Bahama greens. Definitely oil. Or acrylic. Putty? When I went close to read the tag, I saw these were called "drawings." They were inked!

Was this how a person could draw with ink?

At the desk in the back sat a clean-shaven man in a short-sleeved button-up shirt and well-designed hair. I found my nerve and asked him if I could talk to Bettina Dillinger.

He tilted his head and said, not nicely, "Who's asking?"

"Ror."

"Ror who? And what is this about?" He wouldn't meet my eyes but looked beyond me, at the swank people in the hushed space.

"Just Ror. Jonathan sent me."

"Jonathan who?" he asked, his voice like he had work to do.

"Go ahead, tell her," I said. "Tell her Jonathan sent me."

He glanced at his desk, the log book there. "What is this Jonathan's last name?"

"From the frame shop, Jonathan. I don't know. Jonathan, you know."

He pursed his lips at me and lifted the phone and tapped in some numbers. It rang in the back. He whispered into the receiver, and I turned away, my face flushing so hard I could feel my heartbeat in my eyes.

"Go." He hung up and waved to a doorway behind him.

I went back into a white room, a long black desk with chrome legs taking up the length of it. Three Warhol prints of Marilyn Monroe hung on the wall. A short, plump woman about Ma's age, her brown hair in a tight bun, stood at the desk, leaned over a lit-up box. She seemed to be looking at rows of tiny pictures through the light.

"It's over there," the woman said, gesturing to a painting in a corner without even glancing my way. She wore a coffee-brown dress and bottle-cap earrings. When I didn't answer, she stood straight and finally looked at me.

"What are you waiting for?" she said. "I need that back by tomorrow."

I looked at her. "My name is Ror. You have my watercolors."

"Chip said you were from Jonathan's, for the frame. Make

sure you wrap it well and sign it out with him. Where's your truck parked?"

"I'm Ror. You have my paintings. The watercolors?" I hoped I wasn't as red as I felt.

She looked up at the ceiling, "Ror, Ror, Ror," she said, as if trying to remember.

"I left some watercolors in Jonathan's shop, and you took them."

Her eyes swung to me, acknowledging me coolly. "Oh, yes," she said slowly. She went to a large filing cabinet, pulled out a drawer, and started digging through. "Jonathan's a good man, well-meaning, of course. He's always helping younger artists to get a leg up, though his taste isn't always as good as his heart."

I opened my mouth, but nothing came out.

She found the watercolors and stared at them. "Actually, you're one of the better ones I've seen come out of that shop."

"Is that why you took my paintings?"

She shuffled through them, then said, "You're untrained and immature, but you definitely have a facility with watercolors. They're not so easy to use like this."

I coughed. "I made my own paints," I said.

Surprised, she met my eyes. "Yes?"

"Out of pigment and gum arabic. And honey. The honey makes it stick."

"Oh. Are these homemade?"

I shook my head. "Those, no—those are Winsor Newton. Jonathan gave me the paints and the paper."

"You've made good use of them." She held them out. I reached for them, touched their roughness, looked at their density of color. I didn't want to leave—I had a million questions. About galleries and who ran what and how did a person make enough money to get her family out of a welfare hotel.

"Where do you go to school?" she asked.

"Cady High. I'm a junior next year."

"Do you take art classes?"

I told her about Mr. Garci. "Do you want to see some of my drawings?"

"I don't have time right now." She began to turn away.

I started talking fast. "Do you think I could come back? Show you some more stuff, when I make some?"

She indicated the lighted box full of tiny pictures. "I get hundreds of slides every week from people who want to show in this gallery. I simply don't have time to mentor a child. Ask your teacher for help."

I felt a gathering in me, a small chance like a tear in fabric I needed to push through to get to another side. "I'm not a child, I'm seventeen, and I won't waste your time, Ms. Dillinger. You said it yourself, I'm good. I could be great. All I ask is—just—every once in a while, I come in, show you what I'm doing. That's all."

The bottle caps dangled from her ears like something Ma

would make for luck. Only Dillinger was shaking her head. "I have far too much to do."

I hurried on, piling words on top of words. "I could help you. I built a dome house with my father once. I can move things, paint walls, drill. I know how to use a chain saw." Would she think I was nuts?

Her eyebrows raised. "You're a persistent thing, aren't you?"

I held out the paintings like an offering, a gift. "I'll even give you one of my very special watercolors. A collector's item. I'm going to be famous. Choose one. It'll be worth millions someday."

She met my eyes—this time *really* seeing me—then she took the watercolors. She picked the one of Dado's zeppelin in the trees and handed back the rest.

"I'll come back when I have more to show you," I told her.

"You do that," she said, putting the painting on her desk and leaning over the slides.

"Thank you. You won't regret this," I said.

But she was already absorbed in the light.

I went out, past the buttoned-up guy at the desk and onto the street. I took out my pad and sketched the words on the building, DILLINGER GALLERY. Underneath, I drew what I imagined it might be like to have a show there—my paintings hanging, people looking, the newspaper articles written about me. Bodies swirled around me as I drew. The sounds of the city fell away, and it was just me, drawing. I felt him watching me, a Blake angel from above, whispering—

and then I put my pad away and walked back
into the dangerous world.

ACKNOWLEDGMENTS

Julie Chibbaro

Thanks to:

Most of all, Jean-Marc Superville Sovak, for being the first to show me how to see beyond the surface. Jill Grinberg, for seeing and believing. Jen Hunt, for taking a chance. Sharyn November, for adopting, caring, and transforming, and for raising the bar ever higher. Jim Hoover, for such fresh design. Lisaana Otter, for being a great big sister. My Prague writers workshop, especially Anthony Tognazzini, Alan Thomas, and Laura Zam, and to Shannon McCormick, who gave me the first line.

All the artists who let me interview them for hours on end and lent me awesome books and movies and let me take pictures of their stuff to study:

Billy "Bilrock-161" Harmon (www.rtwplanet.com)

Jay "Braze1" Sayers (www.braze1workz.com)

Ron English (www.popaganda.com)

thundercut: Kalene Rivers, Dan Weise

(www.thundercut.com/index.php)

Karlos "Odessy3" Cárcamo
(www.karloscarcamo.com/home.html)
Dan Witz (www.danwitz.com)
And Armand "Mirage" Herreras, for being real live
inspiration all throughout high school and beyond
(www.historicpaintinganddeco.com).

MAJOR INFLUENCES

THE ARTISTS
Andy Warhol (www.warhol.org). Keith Haring (www.haring.
com). Lee Quiñones (www.leequinones.com). Patti Astor and
her Fun Gallery (www.thefungallery.com). Lady Pink (www.
pinksmith.com). Swoon (www.facebook.com/SwoonStudio).
Jean-Michel Basquiat (www.basquiat.com).

THE BOOKS
The Art of Getting Over by Stephen Powers, *Getting Up* by
Craig Castleman, *Subway Art* by Martha Cooper and Henry
Chalfant, *Trespass* by Carlo McCormick and the Wooster
Group, *Wall and Piece* by Banksy.

THE MUSICIANS
Run-D.M.C., Grandmaster Flash, the Beastie Boys, Blondie,
Michael Jackson, the B-52s.

THE FLICKS (AND DOZENS OF YOUTUBE VIDS)
Wild Style, Style Wars, The Warriors, Dogtown and Z-Boys, Beautiful Losers, early MTV, Andy Warhol's TV, Exit Through the Gift Shop.

For more influences, art, and other fun stuff, and to add your own, visit www.intothedangerousworld.com.

JM Superville Sovak

To my mom, for helping me believe, to my dad, for teaching me to draw, and, above all, to Julie, my love and fiercest supporter.

Julie Chibbaro grew up in New York City right

when graffiti was exploding across the subway cars she rode to school. Raised by artists, she has spent her life figuring out what makes them tick. She is also the author of *Redemption* (winner of the American Book Award) and the historical novel *Deadly* (winner of the National Jewish Book Award, a Top Ten title on ALA's Amelia Bloomer Project list, and a Bank Street Best Book), illustrated by her husband, the artist JM Superville Sovak. Her website is **www.juliechibbaro.com.**

JM Superville Sovak is half-Trini, half-

Czech, half-Canadian. His fourth half is spent making art. His work has been shown at the Manifesta European Biennial of Contemporary Art, Socrates Sculpture Park, and the Aldrich Museum. *Into the Dangerous World* is his second collaboration with his wife, Julie Chibbaro. See more at **www.supervillesovak.com.**

Julie and JM live in New York with their daughter.

www.intothedangerousworld.com